# INDIAN JOURNALS

By Allen Ginsberg

*Poetry*
Howl and Other Poems
Kaddish and Other Poems
Empty Mirror: Early Poems
Reality Sandwiches
Angkor Wat
Planet News
Airplane Dreams
The Gates of Wrath: Rhymed Poems 1948–1951
The Fall of America: Poems of These States
Iron Horse
First Blues
Mind Breaths: Poems 1971–1976
Plutonian Ode: Poems 1977–1980
Collected Poems 1947–1980
White Shroud: Poems 1980–1985
Cosmopolitan Greetings: Poems 1986–1992

*Prose*
The Yage Letters (with William Burroughs)
Indian Journals
Gay Sunshine Interview (with Allen Young)
Allen Verbatim: Lectures on Poetry, Politics, Consciousness (Gordon Ball, editor)
Chicago Trial Testimony, 1975
To Eberhart from Ginsberg
Journals Early Fifties Early Sixties (Gordon Ball, editor)
As Ever: Collected Correspondence Allen Ginsberg & Neal Cassady (Barry Gifford, editor)
Composed on the Tongue (Literary Conversations 1967–1977)
Straight Hearts Delight, Love Poems and Selected Letters 1947–1980, with Peter Orlovsky (Winston Leyland, editor)
Howl, Original Draft Facsimile, Fully Annotated (Barry Miles, editor)
The Visions of the Great Rememberer (with Visions of Cody, Jack Kerouac)
Journals Mid-Fifties (1954–1958)

*Photography*
Photographs (Twelvetrees Press)
Snapshot Poetics (Chronicle Books)

# ALLEN GINSBERG

# INDIAN JOURNALS

## MARCH 1962 - MAY 1963

NOTEBOOKS
DIARY
BLANK PAGES
WRITINGS

**Grove Press**
**New York**

Originally published jointly by Dave Haselwood Books and City Lights Books, San Francisco, 1970

First Grove Press edition published in 1996

All photographs copyright © Allen Ginsberg

*Printed in the United States of America*
*Published simultaneously in Canada*

Library of Congress Cataloging-in-Publication Data

Ginsberg, Allen, 1926–1997
    Indian journals, March 1962–May 1963 : notebooks, diary, blank pages, writings / Allen Ginsberg.
        p. cm.
    Originally published: San Francisco : Dave Haselwood Books, 1970.
        ISBN-13; 978-0-8021-3475-2
        1. Ginsberg, Allen, 1926–1997—Notebooks, sketchbooks, etc.
    2. Ginsberg, Allen, 1926–1997—Journeys—India. 3. Poets, American—20th century—Diaries. 4. Ginsberg, Allen, 1926–1997—Diaries. 5. India—Description and travel.   I. Title.
    PS3513.I74Z472   1996
    818'.5403—dc20
    [B]                                                              96-20912

Grove Press
an imprint of Grove/Atlantic, Inc.
841 Broadway
New York, NY 10003

Distributed by Publishers Group West

www.groveatlantic.com

11 12 13 14 15    10 9 8 7 6 5 4

Dedicated to —

Maurice Frydman who said stop going around looking for Gurus,
Swami Shivananda who said "Your own heart is the Guru," a
Mohammedan Baba in Bombay who kissed Peter Orlovsky,
H. H. the Dalai Lama who asked "If you take LSD can you see
what's in that Briefcase?" whereafter Gary Snyder chanted the
Prajnaparamita Sutra in a cave at Ajanta, Sri Krishnaji disciple
of Meher Baba who performed vow of perpetual silence sweetly
declaring all was well without his further talk & that silence
would be good for America, Asoke Fakir who led the way to
Nimtallah Ghat, Swami Satyanda of Calcutta who said "Be a
sweet poet of the Lord," Gopinath Kaviraj who said "What you
are doing seems to be well," Kali Pada Guha Roy who replied to
my doubt of Poesy as a discipline fit for the Void by saying
"Poetry is also a Saddhana & Yoga also drops before the Void,"
Srimata Krishnaji and Bankey Behari of Brindiban who urged
"Take Blake for your Guru," Dudjom Rimpoche N'yingmapa
Lama in Kalimpong who sucked air through his teeth in sympa-
thy calming my fears of LSD hallucination and advised "If you
see anything horrible don't cling to it if you see anything
beautiful don't cling to it," the unknown Nepalese lady-saint at
the Magh Mela in Allahabad 1962 who sang Hare Krishna
Hare Krishna Krishna Krishna Hare Hare Hare Rama Hare Rama
Rama Rama Hare Hare so sweetly I remembered it thereafter,
Shambhu Bharti Baba who motioned me welcome to sit and
smoke Ganja with silent Abhya Mudra in the Burning Ghat at
Benares, Citaram Onkar Das Thakur who advised quitting
onions meat sex cigarettes in order to find a Guru by repeating
the mantra Guru Guru Guru Guru Guru Guru three weeks
continuously (and also said "Give up desire for children,")
which let to conversation on bamboo platform in Ganges with
Dehorava Baba who spake "Oh how wounded, how wounded!"
after I fought with Peter Orlovsky.

— Allen Ginsberg
May 7, 1968

*7 November, 1961* —

Dream, after week of unhappiness and mood arriving by Ship
on the Shore and walking along vast boulevard by Sea, Street
of Lucknow Chickens in INDIA — first dream of India — huge
red and brown night boulevard by water, I walk alone several
miles in night along ox-meat market street till I go thru fairy-
land gate to the Rashbehari Rich Section with modern Apartments on the Seaside — a beautiful front street rich waterfront
like vaster Chicago — I wonder what city I'm in, I'm deliriously
happy, it's my promised land (I'm writing this in the promised
land) — the night street has few people, I see chain of lights
like Riveria hotel facade facing the ocean — I'm coming to a
big church front — at last; it's the Sign Christian all India
Church — fantastic Door, just made for me

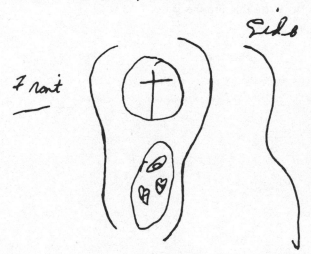

in concrete, like a blind one-eyed skull, with Sacred hearts in
the bottom concrete declivity — as I bend to kiss the S. Heart,
I read the Funeral inscription — "Well it's too bad but good-

by" — I feel happy, it is like a sign thru death here for me — the cosmic joke's come true in happy way — the wonderworld where Man knows he's in a dream — I pass on to a square where with big candles the bodies are on display on wooden scaffolds, covered with white sheet & guarded by Army soldiers in White — I'm amazed by this street display — Next I realize this front Street is only the thin layer of money people, but there are great probably cheap apartments for rent here — I'll settle down like Gregory in one, with my own kitchen, and a white suit, and live free — Then behind these streets must be the filthy hovels I'll explore, I'll walk there tomorrow, I shiver with fear and say, The Bombay seems endless, I never realized how it would feel, first those nites of old city waterfront, then the Great All India Gate to the New City I'm in now which goes on miles too — here's a big hotel, I enter later & get lost in green lobby-garage — I'm wandering in India, it's like a new earth — I'm happy — I wake — Morning in Haifa, my ass aches from a colitis or clap or Amoeba — morn light — time to get up soon it's 6:45 — light to write this prophecy by.

*March 19, 1962, 3:30 AM — The Left Hip*

Visit to Delhi O Den — Classic alley with broken down old Palanquin made by a street charpoy (bed wove on rough wood frame) cover'd by miniature tent, with flap open and grizzled thin fellow attending two huge transvestite Eunuchs in red rags & veils who swished up to buy a spoonful — and we in an adjoining foyer door, human stable, up the smooth wood ladder to loft-platform in the dark, a small shelf cubicle with the mustached serious cook crosslegged tending a flame in a bottle covered with donut holed cap — spinning amber bubbles of O on the tips of iron needles, droplets lifted from a broken teaspoon of black liquid — twirled over the fire, near burnt, dipt back in the spoon, twirled & bubbled again till a gnoblet drop is formed, and laid aside for use — till the moment it is lifted, fired liquid, and stuck in the tiny hole of door-handled size pipe bowl — Inserted with needle to fill the rim of the hole & make a miniature donut circle — This held to flame again till bubbled away into smoke sucked in like choochoo train by smoker thru the doorknob & pipestem to lungs & held there deep unmixed with nostril air.

The smoker recumbent on left hip, relaxed on burlap rug of cosy shelf, a few married Indian onlooker friends attending, head resting on cloth over a brick — does nothing but lay out, hold & suck when given the pipe to lips by right hand of cook — whose hands then hold the doorknob down near the flame wick & keep needle attention to the small O hole, clearing it as it bubbles, — and after a long locomotive suck, smoke filling nostrils & throat & lungs — gives a rap on the steel pipestem with disciplined steel needle to say the pipe is smoked thru & time for a refill.

The original O half liquid in brown glass vial, warmed to flame & dropped down into spoon from which operations proceed as defined above — leading an hour or more later (till now from Midnite to this 3 AM) to dreams spun of so fine a gossamer that the threads snapped ere I woke to fix them in notebook. Coleridge's milk of Paradise a description of interior micro-

7

cosmic thoughtful organism in hypnogogic reverie — a long delicious pleasure — unlike eating O or shooting H or M — an assured constancy of imagination and repose — all proceeding from the classical sordid Muslem alleyway in Delhi, where children drag their dresses and wiggle chanting below low roofs & old householders stand in group or sit in doorways in the early night, unnoticing the familiar neighborhood scene & dreamy public charpoy and shabby stoop of local dope fiend. Who pays off the cop each day & has peace for aye. The shopkeeper who brought us there from his nearby dank little 2 room house and mother-daughter cooking chapatties in an ashy glow, thru alleyways & haphazard bazaar stalls round and round anonymous mazes — accompanying us to nearby main street after, to find a 2 seater put-put cycle taxi & send us on home overawed, relaxed & joying in an older novelty.

Thousands of scenes like this in India I haven't writ, but saw.

*Dream 19 March 1962*

. . . Slowly the whole cabin moves upward on a hillside, I look back in the rain and see we're moving upward on a track, pulled by a wire like a funicular — I worry if we'll fall backward but am assured it is an old tried godly system supported by Eldest Authorities — when we get to the top, I go out searching in the springs cans old rusty car seats & rosebushes thorns for my possessions — I am climbing about on a pile of refuse when a young married couple spies me & says "Ah, this garbage-haunting is what you represent." I sit crosslegged Buddha style over the wires & refuse & bless it and say "I am here to make the Refuse sanctified" and smile cheerfully at the refuse as if it were a big happy religious redemption.

*21 March 1962 — Rapid Morphine Sequence*

Two old men with grey streaked black beards driving up in a horse cab — a finagle whip — sitting side by side for no reason — both drivers, themselves.

An old newspaper seller hysterically waving his papers at the crowds on the sidewalk, selling his papers with a personal combat appeal, "He's against me! He's gonna win!" You got to buy his papers! It's his life or Death! The news he's selling refers to himself and he's a great paperseller because he's got a personal motive and appeals to the sidewalk crowds to be with him in his struggle & buy his papers & read all about it.

A Trotskyite streetcorner lecturer with checkered cap & cape, and bent back, stabbing his fingers into air to make his point, turns round toward you in the crowd — his face is possessed, dark piercing supernaturally intelligent eyes — haranguing with uncanny vehemence & swiftness — no roadside burbler he! — He's a real professional in Hyde Park or 14th St. Union Square — What's he doing here like a unicorn borne up out of opium reverie in Jaipur India RR station bed?

*Jaipur March 25, 1962 — on Morphia —*

Lying from 8 PM to 11 on charpoy (rough rope spring woven on wooden cot frame) in Tourist Bungalow, after spending the day in bazaar and streets Jaipurish —

As lying there in my familiar body, a subtle detachment took place as usual and I lay outside my fleeting life surveying its twinkling away — that now more and more as this life approaches its meridian of 37 years and being half gone by becomes more sure of its mortalism, the chance of the life tho marked by shows and pageants, poetical & airborne — consisting in sexualities & all sorts of fame — as it were — were not much to go by. After all, what's all that experience limited as it is, to a Henry James of the entire Kosmos? So flit as I go by — all I've seen is my own life go by, swift as a mosquito with climactic buzzings of aestheticism & self congratulatory Rhapsody & morphia inactions & musings furthermore. An open closet door — I'll return to the States, take an apartment — where with thinning hair & more tentative soul, arrange my possessions, type up my notes, discharge them for posterities, place my statues in order — one Japanese scroll of medium

9

quality, one Korean print of an awakening Roshi, several cheap Nepalese tantric small figures, Tara, Avaloketesvara, the 1000 armed Destroyer of Death, Ganesha with a red belly button, Hanuman Pious & praying, Krishna fluting, Shiva whirling his arms & dancing, Kali with a necklace of skulls on Shiva's belly astride — an orange wool Tibetan Blanket, a few Amazon cloths & pipes, a Mexican basket, a straw hat and whatever other Persian type miniatures I collect — and that's the accomplishment of a life searching and travel wherever I can go on my earth.

Kali, Durga, Ram, Hari, Krishna, Brahma, Buddha, Allah, Jaweh, Christ, Mazda, Coyote, hear my plea!

Avaloketesvara, Maitreya, St. John, Ho-Tei, Kuan-Yin, Satan, Dipankara, Padma Sambava — whoever there is — is there ever anyone but me?

Lying in bed in Jaipur on morphine, lone in Denver awake on Benzedrine, flat on my back in Puccallpa wrapped in Death Vines, Valparaiso or Santiago enthralled with atropine — Shamans' herbs or modern Somas absorbed & vomited — not yet comprehended to any Eternity. A mosquito buzzing near my ear again. My face sweating having covered itself with thin film of mosquito repellent.

There is no direction I can willingly go into without strain — nearest being lotus posture & quiet mornings, vegetarian breathing before the dawn, I may never be able to do that with devotion. And if it is a matter of Karma and reincarnation, when will I ever learn? All the saints like Shivananda handing me rupees & books of yoga and I'm no good. My hair getting long, wearing a huge thin silk shirt, useless to perfect my conscience. A smoking habit my worst Karma to overcome.

Ill the other day, my bones in flu or grip of ache, sleeping from 5PM to 9AM with supper break & a few cigarettes & dreams and barefoot it down twice to pee — I didn't fear death or think of it. Maybe that's an improvement.

Self Conscious, I have nowhere to go. Maybe might as well leave it at that, continue to travel and die as I am when I die.

Avaloketesvara, Kuan Yin, Jaweh, Saints, Saddhus, Rishis,

10

benevolent ones, Compassionate Superconscious ones, etc, what can you do for me now? What's to be done with my life which has lost its idea?

If it's a matter of each being has to create its own divinity, far be it from me to know what to do or be. I don't even have a good theory of vegetarianism. As for love & sex, I don't know what to say, Peter sleeping on his side in the next bed, still faithful tho I must be poor company to old beauty. And lying on my own back in the dark, the world just keeps revolving as before.

At least I'm down in possessions to Peter & a knapsack. I still am loaded with Karma of many letters & unfinished correspondence. I wanted to be a saint. But suffer for what? Illusions? The rain, were it to rustle the leaves, would seem more friendly than before & more reminiscent of an old dream. But all the connections are vague, machines make noise & lights across the road I've never investigated. Next the rest of India & Japan, and I suppose later a trip: England, Denmark, Sweden & Norway, Germany, Poland, Russia, China & then back home again. And that'll be the end of that world, I'll be about 50, the relatives'll all be dead by then, old ties with the boys of yore be loosed or burnt, unfaithful, in so many decades it's best to let it all go — is Jack drunk? Is Neal still aware of me? Gregory yakking? Bill mad at me? Am I even here to myself? I daren't write it all down, it's too shameful & boring now & I haven't the energy to make a great passional autobiography of it all — for who's all that autobiography for if it doesn't deliver heaven or reasonable equivalent? Anyway, who is that autobiography for? Young kids after the movies? I guess I have nothing to contribute to general edification by this vague haphazard slow motion death. "Red Cats" a fine title anyway.

*Noted on edge of Bombay map —*

Stop trying not to die
fly where you can fly
What do you want to know about your mother?
Anything that gets you high,

eat an orange with your eye,
any movie you see is as good as any other.
It is your business what you buy
Picture postcards apple pie
                    aren't such a bother —
Upside down the birds are floating thru the sky.

*May 4* — Eyes closed,

    Thinking about Phipps —
    Lightning flashes in
    the front of my mind.

Yoga is good for making an entity sit down on the ground &
wait.

# NOTES FOR STOTRAS TO KALI AS STATUE OF LIBERTY

*April 62 — Bombay*

The skulls that hang on Kali's neck, Geo Washington with eyes rolled up & tongue hanging out of his mouth like a fish, N. Lenin upside down; Einstein's hairy white cranium. Hitler with his mustache grown walrus-droop over his lip, Roosevelt with grey eyeballs; Stalin grinning, Mussolini with a broken Jaw, Artaud big eared & toothless; the subtle body of Churchill's head transparent & babylike; an empty space for Truman, Mao Tze Tung & Chang Kai Shek shaking at the bottom of the chain, balls with eyes & noses jiggled in the Cosmic Dance;

Michaelangelo's flayed empty skin hanging from one of the whirling arms, and a huge goddess eye looming over that in its eyebrow oval —

A huge bottomless throat and a great roar of machinery chewing on these Hydrogen Bombs like bubble gums & bursting all over its mouth as big as the Lincoln Memorial —

And a great bloody tongue licking it back into her teeth made of white radios —

Left eye rolled north to watch the planes gliding in the grey heavens above Dew Line —

Right eye in the third head afix on the helpless body of Allen Ginsberg writing a poem to transfix his human image in the goofy cloud of his brain —

Hanging from her ears the jewels of Don Juan & Heliogabalus, the ears of the fifth century head which prophesies & hopes;

The Chakra holding hand, like Whitman's goddess in the kitchen holding a railroad engine's giant wheel, hissing with escaping steam —

The Vajra Hand balancing a high Rolls Royce on end, fenders sticking up into the empty night heavens —

battleships dangling from an arm bent in the bow & arrow gesture — it appeared from nowhere as tho arm snaked into place in the aether —

She leads a separate cultural life of her own, her left hand doesn't know what her right hand is doing

(unbeknownst to each other they both juggle the bones of Sri Swami Bramachariananda)

Rays of Schizophrenia streaming from her lousy forehead in every direction thru the myriad human worlds & looks like shocking pink in this;

And Gandhi bald with a swathe of white cloth Khadi stuffed in his craw — next to Max Planck & Wittgenstein & Trotsky's visages thudding against her Shoulderblade Gefilte Fish skin —

O Elephant Head God Ganipati, appear & disappear for an instant in the mind before I begin to understand the Poem — come save me with your Ray — Better late than never!

King Wenceslas' arm hanging from her hip, next that arm of Thelonious Monk to be, black skin rutted with worms like coral, and La Traviata's swan-like arm & Carmen's all bangled & Gertrude Stein's writing hand covering the gaping yoni, nervously fluttering on account of the Kalpic Dance, which keeps everything moving and makes no difference where it began: Power is a Nightmare

But only the same bullshit substance as a faggoty dream or wedded reverie —

Her Foot is standing on the godlike corpse of Uncle Sam who's crushing down John Bull, bloated himself over the Holy Roman Emperor & Mohammed's illiterate belly, & Moses underneath hidden in a mass of hair, thru which peeps Adams Forelocks & rosy cheeks —

Old Adam separated from Eve who hangs like a Jewel in the artful Nose of this Lady Nirvana —

Violins are playing in many hands, and hands reach out to honk the bulbous horns of all the autos of Bombay, more hands reach out to pull the nets in from the dark ocean

Writing with impossible fish — Here's one with the Head of Jackie Kennedy, and then Mme Furtseva swims into being with her hot body — freed in the thaw — only for this poor dreamy catch — Here on the shore of the ocean sits my dream, Kali as big as the parachute jump at Coney Island, at first glance —

Covered with copies of Time Magazine & India Illustrated
News, her sexual skin — William Randolph Hearst's bones are
circled in a mystic ring on her right second toe —

Earl Browder's Cancer shining inside her left breast with
translucent ghostly light —

I can see it all coming, the 1964 Elections flapping in her left
nostril — If she sneezes she'll destroy the Western Hemisphere

Watch out, don't make waves, choose the third door which
is neither noisy or silent,

Let go, stop trying to compete with God, Creation's already
over, the rest is in the magic stars, let your own mind disappear
the way it wants & usually does

Stop seizing control of the Universe, it already belongs to
your Wife, let her go on gossiping & playing mah jong with
her astrolabes

It keeps her mind occupied especially when she combines it
with rhythmic breathing exercises and Self expressionistic in-
terpretive dancing — put on your pipe & slippers & eat your
eggs by the fire — you can take yr pleasure with her later in
the night when it's dark & the bedroom gets under the covers
with nicotine coughdrops —

When the ear gets disconnected from the brain, you still hear
the noise, but who can remember what it means?

There's nobody on the other end of the telephone she has
in her top hand, she's talking to yourself —

Will somebody please answer the phone? And tell him it
makes no difference what time he gets to the funeral, the under-
taker will take care of the details and somebody else will pay the
bill, & somebody else will play music & somebody else will
pray & everybody will forget it as fast as it takes for the vultures
to clean up a corpse on the Tower of Silence that will be five
minutes and extra charges if you still want to go on talking —

Unless you got wrong number or an in with the phone company which is hardly worth while because her 7th hand is sign-
ing your expense account in front of your eyes — and her 8th
hand has a noose for Pat Brown & Caryl Chessman — one is
empty, one is running for election last year over and over again

15

— and her 9th hand is patting Kit Smart on the skull and tape recording what everybody says for the Johnsonian blather contest —

Damnit! Poking his cane thru the Sidewalk and swearing at the planning commission.

## H*Y*M*N* T*O* U*S*

O Mother U.S., Spouse of Europa and Destroyer of Past Present & Future,

they who recite this Anthem formed from the middle & lost stripes and one star from the cloth of your Nightie,

the speechmaking of such whether issuing from their own empty skulls or that of Sir John Woodruffe

certainly makes a noise on the radio and is good for all nervous breakdowns & common cancer — O thou who art beauteous with the beauty of the twilight's last gleaming

O greatest Country of Countries, even should one poor starving Okinawan get to spell your name right, as you like it, or even form your alphabet in even the wrong combination — O thou who hast great & formidable eyebrows of spiritual money — who bearest on thy hair the United Nations — such even Okinawan becomes higher than Jaweh having conquered thy speechless world, authoress of Maya, and charmed countless youthful Hollywood stars with gay disappearing eyes —

O Republic, auspicious Federation of Crewcut & Pubic relations — from the corners of whose mouths two streams of Politics trickle — they who recite the name of thy 28th Star (Omaha!) destroy all thy communists & bring under subjugation all other fascists sneaking into thine own Fortress America!

O Fortress America, guardian of the future worlds, auspicious Blueprint, who in thy nether right hand holds forth a bathroom, and in thy Nether Left the corpse of Henry Longfellow — Who with thy front hand makes the gesture compelling Disarmament & in thy back that which signifies Foreign Aid,

they, O Land of the free with gaping mouth, who vote for you instead of all other countries, or even thinking of you while they

16

vote for Police Commissioner in Israel & Egypt, or in Cambodia shooting guerillas — who recite thy anthem & think what it means — possess the 8 great secret weapons of the League of Nations lost in the palm of their hand —

O Nation full of Cops, whose throat is adorned with skulls of Rosenbergs, whose breasts spurt Jazz — mid Electronic Sound — in the robot face of all thy worshippers, the recitation of this poem will bring them abiding Protection Money & Pacifist realization.

O Ideal Democracy, even a dope sees Eternity who meditates on thee Raimented with Space, thou crosseyed creator of the Modern World, whose waist is a beautiful belt made of numberless dead Indians' biceps mixed heroic negroes' deathless teeth grins — Who on the breast of Jimmy Dean & Patrick Henry, in the vast bedroom of Forest Lawn Cemetery, enjoyest the Passion named Great Jesus the Christ.

Thou who truly praise thy soul, seated in its body as now in the United Nations Ground strewn with lost civilizations, atom bombs, limited wars, the quick of Lumumba, Castro, Chiang Kai Shek, Trotsky, James Joyce, Altgeld Mayakovsky & Jomo Kenyatta, haunted by the female shoes of Kruschev & Stevenson's long red tongue — Those who art youthful, & those pious of eld — are revered even by spies in all places —

If by night thy Devotee, naked, with long unbarbered hair, sits in the Park and recites this Hymn while meditating on Thee, all the while his full breasted girl fills his lap with provincial Kisses — Such, such a one makes all Politicians subject to him and dwells on the Earth like its President.

O Husband of Russia, should a patriot of thee or any country, clearly recite thine & Russia's national Anthem together or mix that with China thy elephant headed infant, Mighty in all future worlds,

Meditating one year with knowledge of the mystic union of Times Square and Red Square, in any Image Whatsoever — with full knowledge of the Eternal Copulation of Nations that manifests in this Age in thee & thine —

and know thee husband and wife — then such a knower has

17

great prosperity & delight in this life,

and holds all great weapons & official secrets in the grasp of his Kodak-like eyes and Telegraphic Brain —

Ah Home of the brave, thou givest birth to & protectest the world of the Iron Age and at the time of thine Hydrogen age dost withdraw into thy self for new penance that earns new powers over entire planets of all futurity — therefore art thou Husband of Russia and Wife of China and Lover of India, Male-female spouse of all sentient nationalities. Ah me! Why then shall I not not prophesy glorious truths for thee!

Ah me! folks worship many other countries than yourself! they are all brain washed & think they are real as you are — but I of my own uncontrollable lust for you, lay hands on your Independence, enter your very Constitution, my head absorbed in the lips of your White House, O Democracy, who dost enjoy greatest bliss from union with each individual citizen, and who hast intercourse with all man, Eskimo, Alaskan, Oklahoman — and dreams of the wild embrace of world masculinity, Russian, Chinaman, African, Indonesian, Mexican, Puerto Rican & all patriots everywhere the same.

O America, Imagewife of Mankind, thou art Earthy Russia, Watery China, Fiery India, Airy Europe & Aetherial Australia. Also thou & these all Subatomic South Americas are but one — Thou art one world, O well meaning! What more Patriotic praise could I offer!

Of thy mercy show thy favor toward me, and all Me's everywhere, helpless as we are before thine as yet Unmanifest Destiny!

By thy grace may I never be reborn! Not American, Chinese, Russian, Indian, Okinawan or Jew — May I and all my I's never re-incarnate but as Earth Men! Nay, not even earth Identity, but membership in the entire Universe! Grant me this boon, Mother Democracy, — as I fuck thee piously in the Image of America, O Formless One, take me beyond Images & reproductions to be thy perfect Spousely Self, beyond disunion, absorbed in My own non duality which art thou.

He O Mother American Democracy, who in the cremation

18

ground of Nations, with dishevelled hair, and Chaplin pants beat & bathless except in the Sweat of Intensity — intensely meditates inside himself on thee, and makes public his secret offerings to thee in Poetry, music or Electrical Engineering — he alone may know thy cosmic bed.

Know everything about thy Inner America and know all Americas like one big you-me.

O America whoever on Tuesday at midnight, an hour lost in the busy world week, having uttered "My Country tis of thee," seriously even dedicate one cunt hair of patriotic noise to this Idea,

In a Cafeteria of the great Moscow University Bldg or bathroom of Empire State building —

becomes a great poet, a Lord of the earth, and goes ever mounted on an Elephant to end the Cold War Horrors of thy Maya.

O Democratic Republic, the devotee who having sat down on any piece of rented earth, remembers himself in thee, unmanifest, unborn, and recites his my country tis of thee with the least halfhearted conviction — He becomes on earth the President of every Big Business, and the vitamin ocean flowing with production, and is after death a father of the greatest country in the Universe Himself.

He who at night in Union with the greatest country in the Universe, the one and only country, meditates on thee, O Mother with eyes of delightful movies — will smile gently — floating on the breast of a corpse-like America, really entered in Amorous play with the United States of the Universe — becomes himself the destroyer of Russia & China too.

O Black Country, Industrious & modern in every way becomes the Patriotism of any living American Citizen who freely sacrifices to thee in worship his most precious passport, his greatly satisfying Identity cards, together with the hair and bones of his cities, states, national offices, special interests, nationalities & separate dictatorship.

He O Democracy who eats his own laws & sharply in Meditation on thy left Russian foot & Right foot American, and thy myriad other public extremities and private parts — and rightly makes up myriad national anthems to thee every day, and at night when united with his Presidency in bed sings these National anthems another hundred thousand times, becomes I swear on earth like the Successor of Adolph Stalin, without even thinking —

O U.States, this oath & anthem of thine is the source whence emanates all patriotic oaths & national Anthems, It sings of thy real self & contains instructions for the worship of thy

Communist breast & Capitalist breast, thy socialist vagina and thy fascist rectum, thy Kadu & Kanu Innards and FLN's, thy Uretheral CID's and FBI's and all intestinal CIA's and thy also Trotskyite bellybutton.

He who reads it in his living room intently or on the street or hears it over the radio by accident becomes the Daughter of the American Revolution & first flower in pants elected by Politics.

Numbers of Citizens with large eyes, like those of Cinemascope, follow him around impatiently giving away their autographs — Tycoons of Cobalt & Uranium even join the party — An enemy fears him like nervous breakdowns — Living in continuous bliss the Great Patriot Enters the United States of the Universe all at once in his own body, and is never again to be exiled or deported.

Here ends the National Anthem by Allen Ginsberg, entitled H*Y*M*N* T*O* U*S*.

*Bombay 29 April 1962*

Mice running on the streets
of Bombay (a grey mouse streaking
behind a shoeshine box).

———————

Sign "Fraud of a Budget"

Help Discourage Handouts
to Beggars: aid your govt.
[Sign on a collection box]

Shankara said existence is a wet dream: *The Century of Verses* #36

> Self = Man
> Illusion = Woman in Dream
Manifest Universe = Discharge that soils the cloth.

*May 8, 1962*

*DURGA-KALI* — MODERN WEAPONS IN HER HANDS
Kali Yuga 432,000 years — Deity Black
Ten Arms — Borrowed from gods to kill Buffalo Demon —
Vishnu's Chakra or Discus — $E=Mc^2$
Shiva's trident — pitchfork for tossing the hays of mind — Jet
> airplane
Varuna's conch Shell — air Raid Siren
Agni's flaming Dart — Napalm Bomb, electric chair
(wine) Vaya-bow — a gyre of Hot Air & Commotion
Surya-quiver & Arrow — Mass Media & gossip Constitutions
> & Charters & Law
Yama's Iron Rod — Concentration Camp — Buchenwald —
> Belsen
Brahma — Scroll — Religious & Bibles & Laws
> & Registers of Deeds &
> Property Rights
> (fixed Verbal Ideas of Death)
Indra's thunderbolt — A Bomb etc.
Kubera — a club — cop's nightstick, a policeman
Viswaharma's battle-ax — a building wrecker ball
> (drawing)
Sarandra's precious stones & weapons — floods, dams,
> reforestation projects,
> Boulder Dam,
> Dnieperpetrovsk Power Plant,
> Aldermasten & Los Alamos
Milky ocean, a necklace of Pearls — Money & Dollars
> Rolls of Bills & Banks
> from the ocean

From Himalayas — a Lion Vehicle — Roaring
                                    space ship & auto
Ananta — a wreathed circlet of Snakes — belt of politicians
        Infinity belt —                    Mathematics

— — — — —

Greta Garbo's Face on Durga
Nails & Claw like Scimitars
Head! Crowned with Washington Bridge & UN Bldg.
Body! Jewels — Electric lights covering all her
                        body outlined by Neon
*Kali*
Sacrifice antelope, Rhinoceros & Birds
human flesh 1000 years per human, especially
    the head, as well as blood
            *Kalaratruya Mantra*
    Kali Kali Devi Rajaswari
    Lawa Devadayai, Nahah!
    Hrong! Hring!
    Spheng Spheng.
Kali's insatiable blood thirst caused by eating
    too many Armies (Asura whose blood
        drops formed innumerable Asuras)
    Killed him with a spear & drank drips of blood.
Black, half naked. Claws.   Tusks.   Garland
    of skulls, red tongue & mouth
    dripping blood
Shiva = Destruction devouring time = white
Kali triumphs over white time — "abysmal
    void"
    Dance madness. Stepping on Shiva she comes
                                down again —
    theres nothing left to dance on
Kali as Statue of Liberty starts moving
    with ten arms
        reading counterclockwise
    1) High above her head one hand clutches
        Theory of Relativity E=Mc² torch

22

                    sparklers illumining
                Manhatta's boys —
        (one arm holds a bank-watch, rolls of bills
            Pouring out of Colossal windows)
2) one the first roaring Rocket ship of Dr. Huer
3) one air Raid Siren howling into the ocean
4) one Electric Chair lifted above Wall St.
5) one Mandala of hot air, an invisible globe in the
        center of which is a microphone on a TV Screen —
6) one hand covering her pubic hair with Belsen, black human
        smoke pouring from her thighs —
    a policeman doing his duty with his face averted
            committing suicide with his service pistol
7) one hand holding the Empire State Building
    one holds the Holy Books — huge tumbled Koranic
        pile of Zend Avesta, Testaments, Granth Sahib,
        Gilgamesh, Vedas, Sutras, etc. Topped by Book of
        Dead & US Constitution wrapped all in Declaration
        of Independence
8) above that the H Bomb like roary golden Flower
9) one hand holds Dnieperpetrovsk Power Dam
            — Grand Coulee dam in
            the palm of her hand
10) one hand fingers her pearly shining necklace of skulls —
        Hitler, Mussolini, Roosevelt, Chamberlain, Lavalle,
        Stalin, Mayakovsky, Hart Crane, Yessenin, Vachel
        Lindsay, Virginia Woolf, Poe, Dylan Thomas, Ramana
        Maharishi, Naomi Ginsberg, Uncle Max, Aunt Eleanor,
        Uncle Harry & Aunt Rose. & WC Fields — "skull rosary."
11) Sitting on N.Y. IRT Subway Train
        with the Bronx Zoo wrapped around
            her waist
        Greta Garbo's face pasted with Charlie
        Chaplin's mustache & a self-portrait
        Rembrandt eye & her
            Fingernails are the O Sounds
            Escaping from a Blackboard

                        23

        & her body is covered with networks
        of electric Xmas lights outlined by neon —

"If you're interested in the Baroque"
Look at the Statue of Liberty 10-armed like Mahakali.
          * * *

I
    am
        traveller
            eyes
seeing
        this Worlds Fair
            Eiffel Tower 1879
By the blue Riviera sea:
            Late night Galilee
Hippopotamus mudbank riverbend
        boat dormitory window
across wavy ocean end
        a brown hand on the railroad track
with no body there —
I am this
        ten armed Durga
red tongued Kali
        movie of Elephant
headed gods — Ganesh
travelling thru space
always the same place
        There is my movie
I am everywhere
        there is to see as a tourist
or off beat in silence,
        detached from the train
        Watching the moving plain
      Feeling a headache pain
      in bed at night: an airoplane
      humming overhead
        in my ear
        or outside my window

Year after year
I have been here.

*Dream: May 10, 1962*

A toy dog, transparent, made of blown glass — barking &
cavorting — it gives me a crawling heart to realize the dog is
not alive and thinks it is: that the dog is barking Ignorance.
  Dreamt after reading Maharishi Ramana

*Darjeeling May 28, 1962*

Visited Ghoom monastery, sat in prayer hall an hour listening
to sutra chanting — interspersed with horns, cymbals, drums,
bells the great Tibetan sound as on the Artaud tape — sat fixed
eye on water drop on floor & went into "blissful awareness of
all around" — that is a kind of Euphoria with my body relaxed
crosslegged & eyes fixed & mind happy & aware of the long
trail from NY to Tangier to that spot of wet on the floor — also
the clouds outside — also the visitors trooping into the prayer-
hall & seeing me sitting there strangely fixed — also the monks
who acknowledged my presence with several cups of classic
buttered tea.

\* \* \*

Visited smaller monastery & talked with English Lady Lama
who said "of course it's all illusion" when I mentioned hallucination heavens & hells. Sister Vajira.

*June 1, 1962 — Darjeeling*

Woke, disembodied feeling in the mist outside window pen of
small room bed I have — Darjeeling 4:30 AM light, fog —
Chirip of birds & first crowcocks — remembering dream suddenly nostalgic about L.... My 37 birthday coming near, as
"Sister Vajira" reminded me yesterday at Bhutia Basty monastery, asking my birth-date astrologue. I had forgotten, having
remembered a month ago. And wasn't the first youthful body

25

meeting lovely, as strong a thrill as any God apparition?

Yesterday all afternoon tea with monks with crushed noses — talk with Vajira about Initiation — just for kicks — this morn to Kalimpong.

*June 1, 1962 —*

14 years later I'm still being murdered by "God." Om Mane Padmehum.

*June 2 - 3*

Hum. Auspicious. Third night in a row I killed someone in dream. I think, last night by making him swallow a Tibetan skull-chopper — one of those dorje-choppers the Horrific Beasts are always waving.

\* \* \*

Also in morning woke from dream a la Harry Smith: In small town high Himalayas, I see the dromeport Areo Spectacle of fully half only of the earth below, when the mist clears — it's smaller than I thought. This much I do see tho.

*Evening June 3*

Spent all day in pursuit of Wung — Dorge-jig-me's wung, Yamantaka's "Shes" Wung Initiation — from Dudjom Rimpo-che, psychic head of the N'Ying ma Pa, living looking like a woman — like an American Indian with hair done up in bun back of his head, and Tibetan Skirt — He has asthma, gave me a scarf as I left & said come back September & it will be done.

Then lay back in Dharmsala cell on wooden bed & read rest of Harrar's book 7 years, ending feeling sad.

Lay in dark, rain monsoon lightning over after clear vast sunset in the mountains — as I lay just after closing light I realized that the dream of seeing half the world referred to my birthday. For, the remembering my own prophesy desire years back, I always wanted to live to be 74, and I am 37 today — at

74 to see the year 2000. So now I have seen half the world I am to see, & that is written in the bible of dreams.

*June 8, 1962*

Slip Slap Slup slop slutch — walking in the mainstreet of Gangtok in rubber sandals after the town gone to bed — living in flophouse, frustrated, only 3 days pass to stay. Horses clopping outside in the rain, walking the streets alone. Immortal or deathless streets.

*June 1962*

1950's USA —

Compromises of Expedient dictatorships:
    in Pakistan, in Formosa; war in Laos, in Spain, in Argentina,
    in Peru, in Guatamala, in Persia, in Portugal, in So. Korea,
    in Philippines — I saw Roy Howard & that Philippine Politi-
    cian —, in Dominican Rep. Trujillo, in Cuba Batista.

\* \* \*

CHINA

One by one they abandoned the hopesmoke of dreams
turning in their pipes became a formality
By the millions they turned their skin inside out
The rest lined up in front of 100,000 walls to be shot.
There is the Spoken flute the human soprano
Radio Pekin: The age of visible telepathy.

Let my thots run around my head like a bird in an empty box
Mr. Measure is back in Frisco. Mr. Nomad the enquirer is
    retreating before another city.
There are many angles to the cost-plus mandala.
The whisk of squat brooms thru the barred windowside from the
    street 3 flights below.
I am at liberty to tell you — of a horse camel lying on its side
    on the splotched street at nite —
of a mule between the R.R. ties — Black holes where the crows

27

had plucked his eyes out of hairy sockets —
his skin looked as stretched over a wooden drum
an arm, leg, hand, and half the face
        of a man scattered in
        the station at Vrindavan
Where Krishna courted the cows one
        mythology twice removed
May I write some more nonsense?
        Yes indeed please do.
You're on the nod, dear Peter,
        aren't thou on the Nod?
"I'm fantasying Kennedy wanted
        to see us alone so we went
        down an alley together. Kennedy
        was trying figure what to say about
        the Gita. Looked like you were going
        to turn him on to something."
Voices below, and a comb-harmonica
                    * * *

Chapter XI Bhagavad Gita — Visva-Rupa-Dharshana, The
        Vision of the Universal Form —
is what I seen often on LSD etc.
The description is exact objective symbolic
        correlative to the visionary Trancendental Sensation
        accompanied by body-prickles & optical wheels within
        wheels and floatings of the mind amongst
        glimpses of Formless nebulae disappearing —
        whirling within earth-brain.
"Each incarnation is different."
                    * * *

        That's the name of the Chapter and its relation to other
thoughts or my experience. This definite statement of Powers of
these drugs. Is that clear? Can you hear, You?
        Why am I afraid to go back into that Creation? Afraid it is a
3-D delusion I'll enter & never get out of.
        Because I am still clinging to my human known me, Allen
Ginsberg — and to enter this thing means final, complete aban-

28

donment of all I know of my *I am* except for this outer-seeming
otherness which requires my disappearance.

To be afraid to enter is a terrible fate.

The echo of being afraid to be born, to leave Naomi's womb,
even — a sort of hint of pre-natal mortal memory.

Is the same as being afraid to leave the womb of life & go
forth into the State of Death.

All the old religious songs counsel acquiescence.

All the familiar world counsels renunciation of that vision of
Death & rebirth — as a hallucination.

The Tibetan Nyingmapa Lama says: Watch the wheels within wheels but don't get attached to anything you see. Let it pass
into you, but be in-active and not grasping nor rejecting.

Let what happens, happen, on all levels.

O but the Gnaw of dread at becoming that fearful Allen in
the face of that monster, that made Arjuna fall on his face &
pray for his charioteer to take on his old familiar human shape
again — and stop showing all those implacable inhuman gnashy
fangs.

And Great Gnashyfang says it's a favor he shows himself in
this dreadful way, to Selected Arjunas. He says he's a friend.
And he says, None shall Escape me.

When will I ever be ready to die like I boasted in Lion for
Real?

And when will I ever turn my attention (here) to the streets
and figures of daily India?

\* \* \*

Heaven: a place beyond shit & desire. Not to be afraid of
anybody or anything anymore.

\* \* \*

What's the thing I fear the most? I don't even know —:

The ogre that goes with the rose.

\* \* \*

An ogre goes with every rose,
a bee sting guards the honey,
Immortality must disclose
Endless death. The sunny

29

youth sets forth a lunar wrinkle.
Poetry runs from prose.
Tibetan gongs make little tinkle
to Buddha's silent nose.

Why do brazen bearded dogs
Guard the Gates of Heaven?
Why do Angels make such fogs
around the Highest Seven?
Because the hells of Paradise
Make all Creation even,
God keeps adding to his eyes
to watch the outside Heathen.

O What an ocean! whoever seeks
the land of illumination:
That is to say, the lifeboat leaks,
hunger is the ration,
thirst is the First and only water;
There is no Salvation,
Eternity gets shorter & shorter
To finish its Creation!

Hey Ho Anonymo
Ruined Ginsberg sang —
only the sun can dew the snow
and opium kill the pang
for opium. It's all a mess
Celestial orders show —
Death is endlessly the less
Alternative to Woe.

*July 6, 1962 12 PM Calcutta*

Any Town will do
any song rising over the roof
isolated in the night

30

when my eyes are closed
any dark skinned melody
snaking into this black ear hole
Come from nowhere gone
with a breeze of morphine.
or the sound of laundry shaken dry.
or the Creak of green shutters.
or a cough. Any sound, anywhere
Put them together & they make
live music — the Cartwheel over
the nose melody of a baloon.
Alone on a bed, you hear best.
Unrelated but music of the spheres
immediately audible one mile radius
harmony of Crickets & sleepy huh's
from third floor windows — one
man walks up the street crying *crink?*

* * *

"As if he had read Wystan"
Yes Wystan, there's a dear, be
quick now. Finish it off and
don't be naughty, don't play
for the snobby gallery of special
friends. Say what you say
you said already more times
than Whatever number it takes
to make a crowd. How high
can you count? One million
three hundred thirty seven
thousand nine eight three.
That's quite a lot, taken
individually but nothing compared
to your squadrillion vocabulary.
I suspect you are perhaps only
a communist briefcase in disguise.

Who screened you for this job? Aren't
we sure you've done all that before
to reassure our bafflement at this
flat prose? There must be more
to the age of anxiety than a silent
prayer in the White Bavarian Kitchen.
Are you cooking bats ear soup. I'm
against killing, is that fat man
going into the bathroom to kill bats
for supper or just take a crap?
Is that other man dying on the street?
What are we doing here in the dead
of night. Didn't we forget Whose
address we were given, and it wasn't
just a literary gent we were
supposed to find At Home on Call?
Our fathers gave out we would meet
them there. So there's no rush not
to be early. Finish your sonnet
like a dear and don't clean up behind.
The servants can do that for us. Or
there'll be plenty of time when we get home.
Meanwhile send me a note where
to go meet you & Him. I forgot
the address that you're supposed to know
if anyone, you're so meticulous
about everything else. Shall we go?

* * *


## FAMILY TROUBLES

My eye sees everything (like the eyeballs of a cow that's but-
chered and it's dreadful), my mouth goes on talking about what
my eye sees but the eye has no tongue to answer back if the
abattoir don't look like the apple tree I talk about. Meanwhile
my ear counts all the invisible clock chimes and cricket chirps,
tho sometimes my eye and ear collaborate on a jetplane or vol-

cano. There my mouth is left out except for an ah that tags along behind. Independently, almost without thinking, my nose scents another realm that makes no noise like incense or is nothing to look at like a fart or you can't exactly taste like the gas of spring fever. My fingers & skin can feel up anything human nearby & plenty vegetable existence in every direction the trains run, but they don't connect with lots, like, all the stars & bodies in Astronomy. So my eyes ears nose mouth and skin are all grown up with independent income like close relatives who eat in the same house but lead lives mysterious to each other, eye wise elder, ear very noisy, nose rather dim-witted, tongue the black sheep full of excuses & my skin very quiet but perfect for boarding house reach. There is supposed to be a sixth of us but he stays upstairs in his room and nobody knows what kind of work he does like he's crazy. If we all went into business together we could make a fortune, but basically we're so far apart it's like we lived in different worlds. The only time we really get together is in dreams upstairs in the sixth fellow's room, when he goes out. Everybody makes sense on his own but there's really very little contact between us. One thing leads to another and we'll all die someday, I wonder who'll inherit all our property — will some solicitor ring up a faraway forgotten relative & say — OK — Somebody's died & left you a lot of universes, you're the only survivor. Or does the bank keep it all in trust, in perpetuity — all those fireworks, cartwheels, perfumes, tapes and skeletons in the attic plus the family name.

Sometimes I have a feeling that one of us ought to leave home & get married on his own, or break away & lead a separate existence — but that would be unheard of, the family couldn't see it that way, they stick together like marwaris, someone wd. smell a rat and they'd start screaming — But that would be impossible, where could any of us find a mate by himself — and even if such an impossible She did turn up from somewhere in the neighborhood, where could they live? They'd have to elope & disappear, — but it wouldn't be legal cause they couldn't find a witness even if they could find a Judge — and how could they support themselves outside the family — There's nowhere

33

they can go — But folk like us are strange and there's no telling what we're capable of till we do it —Any day I expect like it'll be unnaturally quiet at the table and somebody's missing & we see a note left behind — "Mr. & Mrs. Sound (that's my wife you don't know her) are At Home Someplace Else — We got a fine place in a new Development but the utilities aren't working yet & there's no transport here. Come up & see us later, if you can get away. And we're expecting." But what kind of issue could they have, it would be a baby monster like a big helpless Ear listening in a womb? They'd be ostracised. But you can't stop nobody from dreaming. Most likely Mr. Big Mouth do something crazy like that, he's always yapping about free love & free sex and freedom & independence along that line — anyway he got no future hangin out around the house all the time living off other folks lives, telling them what to do all the time — I wonder just what kind of noisy brat he'd spawn up — some kind of only child living in a world of his own.

What if sound went off and eloped with sound? Nobody would know the difference except they had one of the new-fangled wireless radios.

"Tell Mother Nature to stick to her kitchen" said Big Mouth "I got a life of my own." And you knew Brother Ear heard it all. And Touch shook hands with itself under the table. Old Smell didn't know what was happening. Upstairs the crazy one was tuning in to the scene on his Wireless. And Eye myself Winked, cause I could see something big was going to happen at last in the family. And things were never going to be the same again. Mother Nature just didn't know what hit her & she'll go to her grave wondering what she did to deserve children like this. Well its her own fault, if she didn't want things to happen like that she never should have funcked with Father Time. And him, he's so busy running his business he don't have time for his own family. J.D.'s, recluses, hooky players, dope fiends, dumbells, geniuses — he wouldn't know the difference. Besides its best that way, young folks got to learn for themselves & they're maken their own world.

*Calcutta, July 8, 1962*

Peter's Birthday — ate in Chinese restaurant, eggplant & prawns, fish & tomatos, pork noodle vegetable soup all costing 2 rupees 12 Annas (about 44c U.S.) and took walk up Chitpur Ave. to large Mohammedan Mosque — cool dusk, the orange clouds setting behind the brick red structure of the Mosque Castellated at the end of the Avenue — crowds hurrying by, blind beggars, squatting with hands cupped, a cripple within, twisted leg clomping barefoot by, remains of Japanese rubber sandal straps in the muck garbage blackened & crawled with flies & cats, Betel-nut pan sellers crouching in their booths — The Hurry of Nowhere to go, all for a penny — then took tram back to Bowbazaar St. & walked down street & up alley to the entrance of our building down narrower alley passing the familiar puppet-theater sized & curtained bed-shelf in the alley where the familiar Chinese mad woman lays perpetually chained up stairway one flight in the dark — at the top of the stair on the left against the wall the remains of the day's garbage piled on the floor — unaccountably for this is a clean Chinese apartment — down the hall out the left a big brown dog chained to the curtained family door, across from that the double black door of the smoking room, opened as always, with a little white dog asleep on the cracked tile-mosaic brown floor, cool. Not a big room — high, about 10 feet with a single bright light burning over a desk in the rembrandt-brown gloom on the desk neatly piled some Hindu Notebooks, several cigarette cans of prepared chandol, a glass jar full of red string & papers, some Chinese teacups on aluminum teacup, a blue enamel teapot — and hanging above the brown mood desk — old brown the color of grammar school desks — a little coconut oil spirit lamp with a Gold Flake cigarette box cardboard sheath — a dusty calendar, leaf pulled up to date — with a set of dove or crow feathers stuck behind the date pages — a little wood shelf, with a wood box filled with

35

papers crumpled, hung from the wall — a little round mirror against a nail — a square mirror right under a brown framed Chinese family photo (with cousins & brothers passport size photos stuck on the lower right & left corners under the glass) — (the proprietor in China in a black suit with his wife looking chic, & 2 daughters is the main subject). How long ago he come here dragging his monkey from China's open to debate. — Meanwhile a big blackened tea cup hangs lone on a nail on the mouldy smooth concrete wall — and some other grease-blackened paper, stuck in a tin office paper-vise nearly hangs — presumably, ancient hophead records, unpaid debts from Hong Kong to Calcutta, nobody's looked for years.

One barred shuttered window with a few cans neatly stacked on the ledge on one side the desk — on the other side the barred window open, a few rags & tea pot & crumpled papers arranged between the bars — outlooking on the Calcutta alley balcony 2nd floor right across the way — above the lean-to where the madwoman sits in chairs —

Meanwhile the main business is enacted on a sort of raised stage, a dais where the Chinaman reclines friendly on a big square of black thin worn leather, reclines on his classical hip eyes open staring at the flame in front of him under a brown cracked glass that's held together by last year's adhesive tape set in a bowl to catch stray fallen pellets of O — set in a square tray with all the other measurements — a few porcelain teacups, a wooden ashtray for cigarettes & any other improbable refuse that might find its way up on that bare stage — another tin (empty) from Gold Flake ciggyboos — more ashtray preparations — a pair of the chef's glasses — and the pipe itself — two feet of brown polished bamboo tipped with umbrellahandle bone mouthpiece, looking like a very delicate polished piece of chinoiserie from whoever's Antique Shop they feature these days — a metal bowl, hexagonal edged with silver & centered with some wood-plastic-metal black Ivory in midst which is the pupil-hole in which the pellet of O is poked to be smoked. The Chef holds the pipe and a thin metal needle like a Turk shiskebab stick — both up to the coconut oil light — and tweedles the

36

liquid O out of a fingernail sized cup, and tweedles it over the fire till it bubbles amber and swells to thumb size — and as it cools runs it tweedled alongst the inner edge of the mate-clay-pipe bowl. This makes a pill-sized pellet, soft, which can be poked right through the hole of the bowl. It's a sugarcane pipe. And so the Chef with his head leaned on a brick or square wood pillow attends his eyes on the fire & works, twiddling & conversing, and the smoker his customer reclines on right hip opposite side of the coconut oil lamp — with the clock between their heads, ticking & a big quart size thermos bottle of unsugared green chink Tea. As it is the clock says 5 after six, Peter is pulling a long end of the pipe — asking for 2 more final ones — bargaining over another cup — sure — above his head a calendar, and other with Nehru & Radha on a bicycle. And the Chef rests one foot inside the knee of another foot in a typical Chinese recline infolded body gesture I recognized as typical the first time I saw his foot curled inside there, resting as in Old Pekin after all day pulling the Rickshaw. Over the head of the throne a brown stained old royal canopy cloth — & a cane hanging from the opposite wall — and 3 or 4 Chinese old friends at a time on the hip or puttering around observing or boiling tea or cleaning pipes or preparing special smokes of tobacco from the silver pipe.

*To P.O. — July 8, 1962*

A whitewashed room on the roof,
on a third rate Mohammedan hotel,
two beds, the blurred fan
whirling over yr brown guitar
Knapsack open on the floor, towel
hanging on a chair, an orange crush,
brown paper packages of manuscripts,
Tibetan Tankas, Gandhi pajamas,
Indian books & a bright umbrella,
all in a mess on a rickety wooden stand —
The yellow bulb on the wall lights up

this scene in Calcutta for the thirtieth night:
The opium pipe an hour ago, a book on my naked lap,
You come in the green door, long western
hair plastered down over your shoulders
from the Shower, "Did we take our pills
this week for Malaria?" Happy Birthday
Dear Peter, it's your 29th year.

\* \* \*

Poetry XX Century like all arts and sciences is devolving into examination-experiment on the very material of which it's made. They say "an examination of language itself" to express this turnabout from photographic objectivity to subjective-abstract composition of words à la Burroughs.

As post-Einsteinean science is supposed to come to the frontier of objective research whereat the research instruments themselves are questioned, the human measuring brain is analysed as far as it can analyse itself, to see how the structure of the brain-mind determines the interpretation of the "outside" universe — now found to be contained in the mind perhaps & having no objective shape outside of the measuring mind.

So painting changes thru Cezanne to tricks of space, thru cubism to analysis, finally thru *Action* to the paint itself as the subject matter.

So music moves from old habitual scales & harmonies to abstract mathematic potentialities unrestricted by human presupposition.

Now poetry instead of relying for effect on dreaminess of image or sharpness of visual phanopoeia — instead of conjuring a vision or telling a truth, stops. Because all visions & all truths are no longer considerable as objective & eternal facts, but as plastic projections of the maker & his language. So nobody can seriously go on passionately concerned with *effects* however seeming-real they be, when he knows inside all his visions & truths are empty, finally. So the next step is examination of the cause of these effects, the vehicle of the visions, the conceiver of the truth, which is: words. Language, the prime material itself.

So the next step is, how do you write poetry about poetry

(not as objective abstract subject matter à la Robert Duncan or Pound) — but making use of a radical method eliminating subject matter altogether. By means of what kind of arrangements of words:

Radical Means:

Composition in Void: Gertrude Stein

Association: Kerouac & Surrealism

Break up of syntax: Gertrude Stein

Arrangement of intuitive key words: John Ashbery's *Europe*.

Random juxtaposition: W.S. Burroughs

Boiling down Elements of Image to Abstract Nub: Corso

Arrangement of Sounds: Artaud, Lettrism, Tantric Mantras

Record of Mind-flow: Kerouac.

I seem to be delaying a step forward in this field (elimination of subject matter) and hanging on to habitual humanistic series of autobiographical photographs (as in the last writing on Orlovsky's Birthday) — although my own Consciousness has gone beyond the conceptual to non-conceptual episodes of experience, inexpressible by old means of humanistic storytelling.

As I am anxious or fearful of plunging into the feeling & chaos of disintegration of conceptuality thru further drug experiences, and as my mind development at the year moment seems blocked so also does my "creative" activity, blocked, revolve around old abstract & tenuous sloppy political-sex diatribes & a few cool imagistic photo descriptions (which contain some human sentiment by implication) —

I really don't know what I'm doing now.

Begin a new page.

Hair.  Bedstead.  Iron.  Resurgence.
  Rock.  Capital.  Indignent.  Psycho.
It is like the word association test I took in Stanford on LSD
with Dr. Joe Adams.   The discrete words meant nothing except
superficial associations, but as words were solid objects which
I had no practical use for at the time.
        A Composition of Elements
Cling! the sound of rickshaw handbells
      struck against the wooden pull-poles,
(this echoes & reechoes thruout Calcutta
      day and nite — always invisible reminder)
by the row of Rickshaw boys outside hotel door in street below.
                        * * *
Now it took all those words to place here the swift sound I
recognise in an instant.
  Well life itself is a composition of elements outside words.

things to be done
1.  Write Grove & Olympia for books
2.  Type S.A. Journals
3.  Finish letters
4.  Read thru Notebooks.

*Calcutta typed note. Hotel Amjadia: on Prosody, after a remark
          several years ago by W.C.W.*

There's no reason why every line must begin at the left hand
margin. A silly habit, as if all the thoughts in the brain were
lined up like a conscript army. No, thought flows freely thru the
page space. Begin new ideas at margin and score their development, exfoliation, on the page organically, showing the shape of
the thought, one association on depending indented on another,
with space-jumps to indicate gaps & relationships between
Thinks, broken syntax to indicate hesitancies & interruptions,
— GRAPHING the movement of the mind on the page, as you
would graph a sentence grammatically to show the relation
between subject verb & object in primary school — the arrange-

ment of lines on the page *spread out* to be a rhythmic scoring of the accelerations, pauses & trailings-off of thoughts in their verbal forms as mouth-speech.

To the reader who wants to know the what-how of his fellow-man Poet's mind, the content is laid out in its naked practical pattern & is easy to follow.

Easier than the arbitrary pattern of a sonnet, we don't *think* in the dialectical rigid pattern of quatrain or synthetic pattern of sonnet: We think in blocks of sensation & images. IF THE POET'S MIND IS SHAPELY HIS ART WILL BE SHAPELY. That is, the page will have an original but rhythmic shape — inevitable thought to inevitable thought, lines dropping inevitably in place on the page, making a subtle infinitely varied rhythmic SHAPE.

*July 11 —*
Ever since return from Gangtok I been sick: first slow cold & yellow phlegm Bronchitis with slight fever, went to a doctor & got Procain Penicillin-Streptomyacin Mix injection — Then my arm hard for several days & slightly swollen, sign of an allergy to the injection: Then lassitude of Calcutta heats & dismay torpor days uncuriously reading & tired of talking to Bengalis — Then at Jamshedpur Bengali Poets Conference a slight kidney attack, had to take atropine injection, and returned to Calcutta tired, still coughing from too much cigarettes — so several days on opium & morphine injected once, and tests for allergy which swelled up right arm worse in protest against minute subcutaneous procaine penicillin, then urine test saying excess phosphorus & calcium (oxide?) in urine, followed by sudden dysentery & bone-weak-tired heat fatigue — so tonite a nice big fix with the last $1/2$ grain morphine-atropine & relaxed now in bed my body feels better & the vision of urinary garbage near Chinatown no longer makes me sick at heart.

In case I die: all notebooks & memorabilia published & unpublished mss. & collection of letters & drawings, as well as copyright ownership of published books goes to Peter Orlovsky as heir & executor in toto.

Allen Ginsberg

Now I had just written this little medical report above —
followed (Peter didn't know what I was writing) by at Peter's
suggestion the old idea that I put something in writing about my
will — this apropos of conversation about him preparing his
book of poems finally, and me typing up So. America Journals —
    When I was feeling around my rectum & felt a BUMP — like
a largeish hemorrhoid or a smallish hernia — and said oh! oh!
What next — So we closed the shutters & Peter looked at it,
hmm-hmm — and said it did look like something — and then
he said "Oh Oh, you got worms, I see two white worms" — So
I spread my cheeks & he extracted two live little moving needle
thin wormies which clung to the cotton & I put them on a piece
of cardboard to Show the Authorities.

*Friday 13 July 1962 —*

Top floor Hotel Amjadia Chandy Chowk & Princep St. Calcutta:
looking out the barred window at sunset & the clouds like a
movie film over the sky with cheap red paper kites fluttering
over the 4 story roofs against the mottled green & orange mists
of maya — down for a cup of tea, the sloppy Moslem waiters
barefoot & bearded in black-edged white uniforms — the clang
of rickshaw handbells against wooden pull staves — bells under
hand cars — slept all afternoon after the M last nite and visit
to doctor this morning — worm pills — & read Time & Newsweek & Thubten Jigme Norbu's autobiography — constantly
the unnoticed details of the going universe outside the room
where in heat & sickness & lethargy Peter & I drowse & read &
browse & sleep — Now it's dark evening time and the reality of
the thousand barefoot street vendors & car honkers outside
visible from both windows downstairs as I sit leg folded under
me in bed — Peter wakes half asleep — "my arm's falling
apart" I massage it it's asleep & feels dead & sweaty — neon
lights in the porcelain & dish store downstairs — half a dozen
streetlights dot-burning the picture — looks like Lima Chinatown 2 years ago — most cars speeding by have red tail lights
— nasal beggar or vendor voices — the fan whirling overhead

42

for the last 12 hours — Everything random still, as any cut up. Burroughs it's already a year still haunting me. I slept all afternoon & when I woke up I thought it was morning, I didn't know where I was. I had no name for India.

*July 16, '62*

Heavy rain at dawn, woke & closed windows — dreamed long dream in New Jersey suburbs, Peter & I in bed & he begins with his hand pulling between his legs in bed & we float out into the rainwater I take over, and say when did you come last & he says, oh about 2 hours ago back there in bed before we floated out into the branchy suburban gutter on the rainwater — we're both in shorts & two inquisitive Indian passersby are standing over us — I realize he's had a phonecall before — He says a couple of kids we know young beat poets are coming out to visit — and the girls too — He says its 'Loen' — "*Whom* did you say it was?" —
The door rattles and old Moslem news vendor comes to sell the Statesman — I get out of bed & make him come out of rain while I rattle shirt pocket for money — going back to this dream — Who was that kid that came all the way to Newark? I realize if you go far enough out of the way people will interestingly come & visit.
Back to sleep, the rain continuing all morning while I read paper & stared out the window & read Buddhist Himalaya book till sleepiness o'ercame my eyes:

\* \* \*

In a large comfortable house in India or Mexic suburbs, as a guest — the house given to me to tarry in, I'm settled down and have guests of my own, a big weekend, some young old humanistic Spanish Civil War Political tigers who are visiting friends, I don't remember whom — perhaps that Jewish So. African friend of Burroughs I met in Tangier —
I have with me two bottles of Hallucinogen pills — the mescaline & psylocybin — psylocybin pills are the new ones, they're like minute candy-coated old style I got at Harvard but their

43

power equal to 5 of the old. I take them out of bottle to separate them — I'm going to take some finally — and will go out with them. I take 1, 2, 3, — that I figure is 5, 10, 15 of the old — very solid dose — can't tell what will happen — now should I take a 4th (that makes 20 of the old) — No that might be too much — anyway I have a good strong dose — I've been carrying the fourth extra in my hand & I go to the bedside cupboard to open 2nd bottle & put them back & keep them separate — If I go out I can carry with me — I leave the separate Mescaline bottle behind — Peter is there, I say do you want any he says no, it's too sudden, my decision, for him — I'm not too scared, I just want to wait & see: I think, well the first result, a new accession of courage — I must stop putting myself down as I have been doing all along the last year. And a sudden flood of straightforward self-confidence. But the actual chemical results of the pills I don't feel yet — My guest friend says he's just painted up a new cream color over the wall at the side of the bed — I look & can't tell much difference except its smoother — he says "I couldnt' bear with that old splotchy leprous rotted painted wall here near my head before" — It's alright by me I think. — I wake up.

First of all this is the first time I remember dreaming about the hallucinogen pills. A neutral dream, doesn't prophesy what my unconscious will feel like when I see it next time I take pills if ever again.

Second, it follows on meeting I had with skeptical think intelligent Jyoti Datta Bengali Poet this yesterday — & coming home after showing him *Aether* I realized how much of my life I'd put into this sort of exploration of mind thru drugs, & how sad & futile I felt now that I had gotten to point with hallucinogens where I no longer liked what I felt & was too disturbed & frightened to continue.

Also last night I was opening my mouth to look at back of throat, & the mere notion of throat opening set off a nervous vomiting reaction. Peter on other hand stuck out his long red magic tongue & I could see (for first time) all the way into cave behind curtains of red skin behind hanging tonsils — the flesh

44

wall mottled with membraneous venous skinny brick color. Then
I stuck out my tongue instead of doubling it in fearfully as I
always do & my own feeling of nausea passed by. This only an
association of nausea that may have impelled the dream.

Also thinking this week, I should write Burroughs I'm still
stuck in the heart by the cut ups & still atrophied back where
I was in Tangier & not moving anywhere.

And I have these pills with me for several weeks now or a
month?

And all this year & last I have made constant reference
on every side, public pronouncements etc & now all my
time is taken up exteriorizing verbally this *idea* of alteration of
consciousness.

But I have failed to alter my own & the means to do so are in
my hand, at least to experience again the sensation which I refer
to to other people as alteration of consciousness. In short I'm
afraid & waiting for I don't know what to push me on. Finally
I do something in this dream.

## MAX FROHMAN

     — of Uncle Max who was a large frail man
I loved, who had a Canadian mustache,
and thru my boyhood slept in bed till noon
So that I never knocked at his door early
lest his heart be disturbed — of his cozy
childless house, and his phonograph machine
where I first heard Bellini & Saint Saens
Introduction & Rondo Capricioso, those
delicate first violin strings' notes few —
prophesy & sad breath. And Elanor who
had died, and my few visits to Max
thereafter, childhood over & my wanderings
begun. And Max stayed where he was,
in the same apartment, drinking coffee
in the noon hour for his breakfast & made
his accounts, went to his office on Subway,

— Last I saw him I visited & read him
poems on the death of Elanor — like
a longhaired vulture, over the table in
his kitchen, we wept.

*July 28, 1962 —*

Now I am brooding on a pillow
with my arm resting on my head
eyes closed open on gulfs black Time —
Water buffalo herds, wide streets,
the liquid image of olive oil
Popeyes in and out of a second
mixed up with the vast blankness.
This is myself in the flesh.   Whom
am I to trust?   I feel companion
to all of us now before death
waiting inside Life.   One big
place we are here.   Others have
left before us — Where could they keep
themselves absent from now — but
what tricks they had to play to
escape from the fat bodies —
to take that step at last, cracked
open from head to foot, choking, blind,
swallowing themselves entire like
the snake that does remain
to them the old Reminder of
before the solitary question
one became one was familiar
— That poor hopeless being in the dark
knowing its own whole universe
a big selfish lie become so
painful it must vomit all its
memory away — and let that
reptilian vastness recreate itself
apart from eye or ear or any dreaded

touching any more — Who am I in bed
with my eyes closed, so familiar
from before — like the Ghost of Elise
running in panic under Bellevue
Gothic arches and dragged forth
into the daylight by her family
the Police — What was she
pointing at in the Hudson River at night,
the voices only she could hear
— and now she is only this ghost
fleeing in the dark halls of my
vast head with its eyelids curtaind-
to. ˙ Now it is Blue dawn outside,
and I'm back in the trance of
smoking & talking across the
concrete room with breezes of
Indian Fan and my hiccups.
I'll be a symboliste.   And Aunt
Rose be a symbol, shining in
Transparent Newark, and Uncle Max
be sitting at his desk adding
up figures on a page like me &
smoking a cigar, and Aunt Elanor
too be in me as I saw her last
lying in Montefiore bed behind
white curtains, frightened schoolgirl
voice say "am I going to die?"
And Uncle Harry, one by one,
upstairs in the bedroom realizing
a cancer while I was far away,
and Naomi now wailing only
in faraway rooms of ten minds
dressing & undressing & pulling
her brown stocking on & off, and
Uncle Sam's big head looks more
dwarfish as the years have passed
him by & Garver's coughing by the

47

barred window, and Cannastra's
showing his bloody hands and I
am amazed by the dead population
that must grow to include me
with the rest.   So what!   This is
all I'm afraid of I guess — as
it dawns that it will make
no difference after I'm gone — We
all will be free from each other
if that's what we want to
escape the nostalgic selfpity
of separation.

*Aug 4, (6 AM) 1962*

Midnight visit from some Illinois Professor who looked like the
doll-like cardplayer in Cezanne — I stared at him thru the bars
of the hotel at 1:20 AM & finally got them open by sleeping-on-
floor-bearer & went out in car with him & Indian Market Research analyst from Ramakrishna Mission to Punjabi all nite
Restaurant.

Wherein ensued an argument he being expert in ethnic lin-
guistics that is music & said he done study of poetry analysis to
find all the basis etc.

Said (in sum) I was getting away w/god too easy with pills
& satisfying elegance naught. So I got mad. Will reproduce the
argument later. Went to bed perturbed. Said I was Revolt of
Sudras (untouchables) poet.

\* \* \*

Dreamed: I met Kruschev who seemed powerful & intelligent
& we got into conversation, about poetry, he putting it down or
slightingly till I talked about Mayakovsky whom he also put
down & put me down and as a parting shot as he left to show his
own invulnerability by the RR. Track — "The music of my
death is blank." I had dallied arguing sophisticated with him
trying to match his information & analysis & he beat me out
& to boot penetrated my heart with this flash at my own ego-

tism's death fear. In dream a dread of Kruschef & increasing anxiety that I was being confronted with omnipresent omniverous center of State Cosmic Controlling agency.

The *Fights* 1962:

U.S. vs Russia in General / China vs Formosa over Possession / India vs. China over border territory / India vs. Pakistan over possession Kashmir — Religious / India vs. Portugal over possession Goa / India vs. Nagas over Independence / Egypt vs. Israel over possession of territory & Religion / E. Germany vs. W. Germany sovereignty / Cuba vs. U.S.A. — Ideas / N. Korea vs. So. Korea — Sovereignty / Indonesia vs. Holland — Territory / France vs. Algeria — Territory / Negroes vs. whites — U.S. / Katanga vs. Leopoldville / Russian Stalinists vs. Russian Kruschevists / Peru A.P.R.A. vs. Peru Military / Argentine Military vs. Argentine Bourgeois / Navajo Peyotists vs. Navajo Tribal Council — Tribal / W. Irian? / Kurds vs. Iraq / Negro vs. Whites — So. Africa — Race / U.S. Senegal vs. Red Mali — Territory / Ghana vs. Togo — Territory / Ruanda Watusi vs. Ruanda Bahutu — Tribe power / Kenya Kadu vs. Kenya Kana — Tribe power / Somali vs. Aetheopia, Kenya, French Somali / Tibet Lamas vs. Chinese Tibetan Secularists / India vs. E. Pak — Aasam Bengal over Border & Tripura / Algeria vs. Morocco over Sahara.

*Internal Friction w/bloodshed:*

Panama / Venezuela / Peru / Brazil / Argentina / Guatamala / Haiti / Hungary / Poland / E. Germany / Roumania? / Greece? / Algeria /
Albania vs. Russia — Ideology / Nepal vs. India — Border Raids.

*Dream (new pen) Aug. 15, 1962 Indian Independence day
    afternoon*

Walking or pursuing phantoms, Jack Oakie or Lama Galwa Karmapa, in evening dress, wandering thru vast schools &

apartments I come on old inner courtyard by kitchen window and kneel down in front of a figure of a man — I had found him & demanded the answer — and as I demanded, I sank on my knees with softer & softer heart & more urgent demand until my demand was all bended knees & tenderness and carelessness & head bowed in silent prayer, and when I slowly lifted my head up the figure had disappeared (and as in a French Raimu Movie as I noticed in dream) in its place (as in Joan dream) was the bright window and light pouring in from the afternoon sun made more rainy-luminous by the darkness of the interior of the room. So the answer was always there behind the man but the man had to disappear for the answer to be seen, and the answer was the light, sunlight, in the window. As Naomi (afterthought) . . .

* * *

The question I asked was, "What is the answer" and I realized as I went on my knees in lightness & carelessness it was better to ask "What is my answer" or "What is the Great Question that troubles me?" for which I received the answer: a lighted window.

I been *demanding* in mental war, and the point of the dream was that the light was outside demands but related to mercy-bliss-tenderness-peace-calm-"spiritual."

*Aug. 28*

To be or not to Be Speech:
Hamlet, if you take up action you'll get killed in it, if not, you'll get killed anyway, surrounded by the hosts of Rheumatism & Cancer and pleuresy & stroke. Either way go into the mouth of Krishna as the armies on the Field of Krushekta (?) — Baghavad Gita. It's a laugh, either way, to be flung into the mouth of life.

* * *

The Zen man hanging by his teeth with no other answer.

*6 September —*

Long walk nite Calcutta streets sleepers on curbs roads in restau-

51

rant lights drank milk tired looking everywhere on the bodies.

It isn't enough for yr heart to break because everybody's heart is broken now.

* * *

Forlorn, the man-vast mystery hanging over us all
The doom of the world in the papers for 20 years sunk in
(daily iron radio voice telling different sides in different tongues
Television where nobody can see a naked man, TV with a hidden
    hand on the switch to keep control if the madman comes
    with dishevelled pants —
Telephones tapped in twenty countries wherever high echelons
    whisper — only in the center of Red Square, talk talk
    talk — )
To each soul, what's left to pray, man become machine
Where bones dissolve, & flesh takes ulcer
And the foot gets dirty in the grave —
Heigh Ho, the fan is whirling and the lights are bright in
    Chandni Chowk —
Tibetan Skeletons dance in the red flying fire —
A breeze blows thru the room —
Peter sleeps in a sheet, with long yellow hair & his cheek on the
    pillow —
And all's well, man lives, and will live ten million years from
    now near a star I'll never see but in a dream.
We have to defend life itself!
   (Echo of Les Preludes of Liszt
     the Horns of Annunciation from the Beyond)

* * *

The lesson of drugs is:
      the experience of the sensation of
change of the physical body & brain,
      change of brain consciousness
        & how it feels to see
        the inside-outside —
          Snake biting its tail sensation
    of the mind changing (the cellular
    switchboard making new combinations

52

So the phone is phoning his
own number —
Whoever picks up the phone is you —)
and seeing if you change the
cellular combination *all* the way
you get the final number
0000- ∞
address: outside
Name: Mortis, Timor
So either you call him & pay the charges
or call up your best friends.
\* \* \*
Jack: Wouldn't want to be allen.
*But:* Wouldn't want *not* to be allen.
Somebody's got to be allen.
\* \* \*
Revision of the *Names*, the trick of superimposition of key
words by cutting out the fat participles & getting deeper images:
Example: "His dream, a mouthful of white prick trembling in
his head"
To: "His dream mouthful of white prick trembling in his head"
\* \* \*
"Which Distance?
Giant size I said
A hole is not the Universe
The Soft —"
from Dream
poem in Typewriter
"Machine creates
its own wrapped limbo into the Beyond
and there is no sad Victory for Human or Ape
if the scissor blindness snips the ears
before the White boys sound the end of the
Trumpets War."
Tea & Crumpets mama, I was walking up the rainy street on
the way to the International Hotel when one of the gruesome
bell boys stopped & took my hand and said "I know a sandy

place" down here below — I was grinning to leave not having
no money nor guts to forbear from my frigid politeness When
he pulled out a crisp new note
that read £5 — five pounds, just Who is that
I looked and he took off his cap & revealed
  a spoilt schoolboy
with tender pale cheeks & a leather jacket
urging me on thru the wooden gate to make love
"I'll do you myself" he said just give the chance
Why not? so I followed & took off his shirt in surprise —
He jumped down the front lawn of the empty flat
  upon flat receding in the valley of boxes
    and windows: I stared
at him down in the garden there & blank windows
where nobody watched.   But somebody watched
yes from the second window a young husband
saw us as burglars.   I waved hello & waited
till my boy friend got the signal & climbed up
over the wooden fence again:   we kissed
while the neighbor sounded alarm to his Wife
and I leaned backward thru garden-wall to pick up his leather
  clothes
When the bastard! he struck me & twisted my neck
He'd murdered me then & there if I didn't fight,
he'd make me a vampire in the old Machine from Before
I remember the last time on this empty street betrayed
So I lifted him up & shook free, and attacked the typewriter —
seeing the words on the page flowing "The soft Which
Distance I said giant size hole in the Universe"
and shook my self woke & shuddered in my dream
To remember the poem & write down, this time perfect the
  dream Poem
Not on the faulty typewriter of the last 2 dreams
but waking conscious pen in hand scribble that lasts forever
  and Ugh! the pain in my head
Ache of my body in bed with no desk
  no poem disappeared

Allen Ginsberg preparing to wash while travelling in northern India
with Gary Snyder and Peter Orlovsky during January 1962

Gary Snyder, Peter Orlovsky, Allen Ginsberg on wall overlooking
Himalayan range vista, Kausani, early 1962

Peter Orlovsky, 1962

Bird seller, downtown
Calcutta, Bombayaar
Street & Princeps
Street corner

Baul Saint, Calcutta
street corner

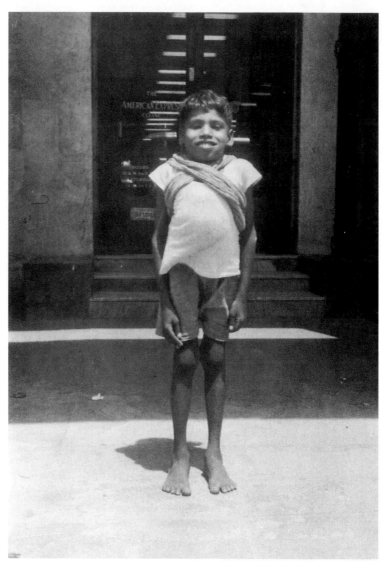

At the American Express, Calcutta

Peter Ganesh Orlovsky at entrance to Amjadia Hotel restaurant,
July 1962

Peter Orlovsky overlooking Calcutta neighborhood Muezzin
chanting from mosque, Choudui Chowh, across roof of Amjadia
Hotel, July 13, 1962

Row of rickshaw boys outside hotel door in street below the Amjadia Hotel, July 13, 1962 (see p. 42)

Transvestite singing at Hotel Amjadia corner

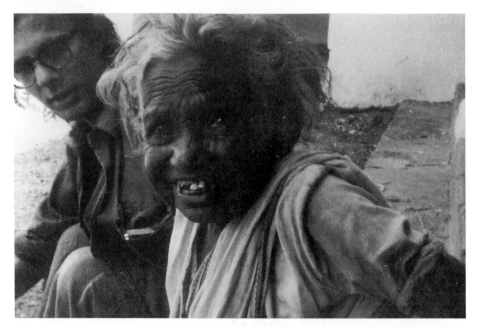

Peter Orlovsky beside old beggar-woman

Bidi (cigarette) shop proprietor across street from Amjadia Hotel, October 1962 (see p. 55)

No sale on the Cash Register ringing
except for the Words:   "Which Distance"
broken off premature on Dawn
    blue lead sky Chandni Chowk
The bastard kid he tried to attack me!

*September*

    Mossadek weeping in Court
1962 Recalled to the Front
Pages
        It all Comes out
        the C.I.A. Him overthrew
because
    His government fell
Because
    He Nationalized Albion-Persian Oil Company!
That dirty board of Directors!
                        * * *
the Acts of Destiny

*Dream Oct 1 —*

Gandhi's Birthday, earlier today dreamt of kissing Peter between breasts, the white softness like a woman. Later he came into my bed for real & his ass felt the same.

*Oct 1? '62*

By tram upper Chitpur road to the Mosque — bought Moslem aphrodisiac, sitting on wooden board-stoop of the shop, gossiping with mustached fat boy proprietor who explained "... For pleasure. If the erection doesn't last long enough ... temporary pleasure ..." Then walked up to Mahatma Gandhi road thru crowds & black puddles splattering my calves, thru a side street to Burrahbazaar & drank a glass of Sherbet (without Bhang) (offered from a small green moist pile on a marble block

55

next to the ice, perfume, & curds) — then wandering uptown North thru park where white sheeted old ladies were curled up beneath the shelter — To left toward Ganges thru a winding sidestreet where big bellied old Bramhan pointed me out from his shop-stall perch — to Nimtallah burning ghats, in the garden groups of squatters ringed around little devotional flower heaps & lit incense & small flames & ground ganja & Tabac in their palms & passed the pipe around — one ashy saddhu in loincloth with long hair & baby-apron above loincloth — thin arms & legs & froggy voice — squatted with rest — circulated group to group — a drum here & there & a blind beggar on the path patting his drum & singing constantly — the saddhu got up & danced around, snakey sex gestures like a burlesque act — collecting money & prasad which he immediately wolfed down with exaggerated self-conscious eagerness — walked around the burning spots — piles of wood red all burned with a long leprous looking foot sticking up out of the woodpile as yet unburnt — then spied a young saddhu in an alcove sitting crosslegged observing the burnings, I wandered over & stared at him but he didn't move his closed eye — out of the smokey ground & alongside the ganges on the high bank huge groups 10-15 men squatting around passing the ganja pipe — smoking with exclamatory prayer Bom Bom before raising face & hands in prayer-clasp on the pipe, eyes to the sky, closed. Wandered into the Mandir (temple) crowded with flower sellers & Saddhus — one young handsome half naked kid sitting next to an old lion-maned white hair orange robed father-saint, asleep for too much smoking — a wildhaired loinclothed saddhu I stared at, & departed regretfully — back to the burning ghat, watched a small child's naked body rubbed with grease & prayed over by Fire helpers —they rubbed their hands with white ghee-grease over the small belly & penis & black haired skull — then lifted the empty body on top of a small pile of thick wood & arranged it there, covered with muslin — arranged the little arms at the side & straightened the feet out, knees resting on the cut wood blocks — That to be burned — and an old prosperous looking man's corpse laid out buried under a blanket of

56

wood chips — his head left free to see uncovered — as the fire burned under his platform the fat grease perspired over his dead face. Groups of men going in and out singing song — prayer — exclamations, everybody high — crying "Hari Bol!" (Tell or name Hari) An orange robed man had offered me a drag on a pipe earlier — the smoke smell of burnt flesh & wet wood acrid as I circled the flames — one fine looking nose in white crosslegged before a burned out pit — and back to the alcove, an older orange robed Tantric had settled there & was preparing to meditate — I went up to the door & looked in — his eyeballs gleamed at me for an instant as I looked inside — big white beard — he snapped his fingers around his head driving away spirits — Closed his eyes & counted ghosts professionally on his fingers — very efficient & habit-rapid — then he seated crossed his leg up — looked at me & waved me away with decisive gesture — I made namaste & departed — walked around again & saw the old man burning, smelt flesh, watched the Saddhu dance, & walked to Chitpur road, took rickshaw at near midnight back to Punjabi restaurant to gnaw at bones & peas & then walked home to Amjadia Hotel.

*Dream, Oct 3, 1962*

8 AM Ringing of hand bells on street outside —
   A tiny babe form, as, wrapped in a leaf — I lay it on a small pillow covered with red cloth, it's the size of a pea — smaller, the size of a grain of rice — I've rescued it but don't know what to do with it — I give it to Jerry Newman-Calcutta Zoroastrean boy to hold — both semitic-eyed — misunderstands & What! — I scream you've messed it up — I take it back it's in two wriggly parts now like miniature cocoons of dough. "You rolled it up like a piece of Snot" I yell, & fling it out of my hands — Can't stand the idea of that life mutilated so small & hopeless in my hands.

*Durga Puja Oct 8-10 1962*

With Asoke Fakir a 37-year-old saffron robed long black hair
negro who looks like my mother walked into my room a
stranger one day — went to smoke ganja in his favorite haunt
"Ganja Park" a square of grass & trees on the side of main road
from Chowringhee to Rashbehari Avenue — streetlight far
away thru the trees & a wet bench. The young caretaker came
our of his hut & served Asoke water. He once saw Kali's feet
pass on the path before his lowered eyes as he slumpt crazy on
the bench —
    To Kalighat — we lay on a marble floor in nearby Temple-
arcade in park, smoked cigarettes & he talked while I lay back
— Then passed to the Kali Mandir inner sanctum & kneeled
& saluted the black three-eyed stone — Then to the burning
ghats, I watched the bust & head of a lawyer turned over in
flame — and two minutes stared in saddhu's eye.

* * *

Dream afternoon — cold in the morning & insect bites on
breast and arm —

* * *

Alas never to know the end of Universe when the last star
folds into the last thought.

* * *

When I was young you came with the
voice of tender rock.
                    Transformed the Sun.
Exact pictures no longer describe.
My poetry no longer describe.  The
Contact.  Dear Blake, come back.
I lay in my Calcutta bed, eye fixd
On the green shutters in the wall, crude
Wood that might have been windows
in your Cottage, with a rusty nail
and a ring iron at the hand
To open on heaven.  A whitewashed
Wall, the murmur of sidewalk sleepers,

58

the burning ghat's sick rose flaring
like matchsticks miles away, my cough
from flu and too much cigarettes,
prophet Ramakrishna banning
the bowels and desires — Dear Blake,
                              Ahch!
Oct 13, 1962 —


    Drunk Bhang at Burrabazaar bright lamp stall, walked to
Howrah Bridge thru Mahatma Gandhi Road, then under the
Bridge, the roar of Earth-machine, a big crap in the concrete
bathroom, watching the wrestlers covered with night time dirt,
then the Sadhu with Lingam pink cone hat, & sitting in bushes
under bridge on the little promontory — then up & Nimtallah
burning ghats walking — only one small fire burning down —
myself in a sick daze — I swore I smelt the Vomit Market nearby — thin ragged beggars with a few Pice & cups coming to
buy the human vomit to nourish themselves — and I began
retching walking past the gate at the burning grounds, then
next the image came I was near the human Meat Market —
and we did soon pass a cow meat market with big cow backs
hanging on hooks — a weak butcher with a small ox hanging
on the carcass, the ax bouncing off — till he cut & severed the
corpse in half as the backbone came in two — the meat relaxed
like worms wriggling opposite — and all that human meat
being severed from the arm and neck — I vomited into my
throat at the smell — & then with Peter walked all the way
back home, stunned & silent.
    Later was told they mixed Datura with my Bhang, thus the
hallucinations.


       *Dream*
A page of Pound:
   i.e. a sunset picture in the dark
   band & cartoon — & a line of poetry in it
"Who made American song who American sung"
Sherri Martinelli

# TO W.C.W.

*(Hotel Amjadia Restaurant, Calcutta)*

Old man,
        the dozen green
bits of peppers in a bowl
on marble table top,
            all the details
I mean all the yellow rice and mutton
in my Mohammedan hotel are yours
      in Calcutta —
    I love you,
        with interruptions
        that flit thru my ganja head
    as Ashok Fakir dips his spoon on the plate.
Concentrated & spontaneous perception
    of continuing particulars,
        I'm no good at that
           too sloppy
    I must admit after all these years —
    "down around the river". . .
All your identity's in your red books
        I read them tonight sighing
All there, from the machines of the 20's
    Them modern steel skyscrapers
        of enthusiastic daylight,
    a torn brown leather jacket
        paper in the insole
Six ladies swishing in the urinal
from the proletarian Thirties
        (I turned to "god" —)
For the Fourties a new sense, Atta boy
        atta boy — death of yr mother? —
    bayonets gleaming in your mouth —
The new world risen into space ships . . .
A stroke "I'll never see you again"

in this garden — But I seen you again
     in the Fifties "Lotsa bastards
          out there — " pointing thru the window
Kerouac drunk in kitchen talking with Flossie
     about old Bavarian beer garden
          dances & 1910 medical Europes —
And I lied to you, told you I was never a fairy
     when I was — didn't want to
               shock yr palsied hand
     on mahagony table pizzerria downtown
          Paterson below Market St.
A walk by the mighty Passaic — a hand
     full of dirt and razors — "This is the poem" —
But this is Calcutta I'm sitting in —
     Your ghost, old provincial
               stranger entering Chandhi Chowk
                    muttering bengali —
     I thought I was your agent-spy
Poor man never saw Ganges never
          bathed — but glimpsed Passaic
               as Ma Kali just the same

          . . . Now time in my room, cell walls rooftop near Mosque
hearing the bearded grocery scholar wail his
     Allah, holler on streets —
I steal out with long hair to find Paterson near
          the Ganges bank Nimtallah burning ghats
               to see the meat-dolls burn,
     spread toes hanging out the end of the woodpile
     face black bone mask with gleam white teeth
          slipped down from the skull-cap
     and yellow-black brain in smoke
               shrinking aflame
     as I pass red walls by the river.

Black steel roof one mile long
 Thundering to the opposite bank
  near the bright blue/Wills Gold Flake
  Bolt of light on Ganges
   waters, and candlelight
 in scows' rembrandt shadow
 drifting below my crosslegged
   view — near the oily
 muscles of Indian wrestlers in nite time
  rituals on burlap mats
   beneath Howrah Bridge —
Roar of tidal bore — wall of grey water
 rushing past the burning ghats

A soft ache inside belly —
I squatted with pained knees
 in the public cubicle near the tram
  car crashes at the bridge causeway —
in the gloom, beneath my behind
 a puddle of brown pudding,
 Someone's untouchable
before me on the wet concrete
 scattered splashes of green feces —
 barefoot they enter & relieve —

The most un-american lavatory
I ever saw was in Dja M'alfna square
  Marrakesh — a circular
  Bomb cellar
 with dozens of reticules
  overflowing with arab excrement
 all over the floor, and strokes
  of brown clinging to the wall,
 marks of the left forefingers
   of Marrakesh!
 It looked like Jackson Pollack
  painting — action, rearguard!

*To Gary in Letter:*

Humans eyes & lips blackened & crackling in flame, hair smelling with human fat dripping from neck as skin turns bright red & burns —

Under the great Howrah bridge, an eternity style bridge with all Calcutta passing over it in bullock cart auto tram bus bicycle or dragging leprous foot —

A sustained wild roar that rises and falls like music, crescendos of Trolleycars and trucks reechoing under the vast steel roof that collects the vast Noise into one vast oceanic crash — Om —

Saddhus sit there on Ganges with Will's Gold Flake yellow & Red Neon shining from across the waters below bridge — just like home, Westminister, Brooklyn —

a cover photo of beautiful small-faced cripple beggar girl sleeping under her black umbrella —

Boys poking the corpses with bamboo poles, a lawyer's shoulders and head seared and puffed up over the flames, pushed by attendants so it falls into the central red coals —

Ten feet away group of saddhus & devotees around improvised mandir with flowers & incense and prasad on a cloth, shouting loud Boom Boom Mahadeva! lifting faces to sky eyes closed hands clasped to mouth as if in prayer, except in their hands little red clay pipesful of Ganja — passing around the pipe with great mantras —

Saddhu dancing to blind beggar's drum on the pathway, thin armed snakey hip sex gestures & slow shuffles —

Eating prasad with exquisite deliberate gesture both hands to mouth wolfing it down & going to the next circle of teaheads to try their pot & prasad.

The corpse smoke rolling over their heads, bodies burning — one of the worst areas of the Bardothodol & demons with long Bamboo poles pushing that meat into the flames.

Lying in bed, one hard electric light foregathering little green flying insect sparks 3 feet around its reflection on whitewashed wall in roof cell of Mohamedan hotel — Calcutta —

63

Corpses heaped with flowers in a litter carried thru streets
... disappear right in front of you like burning a big meat doll
or pillow or Sofa —
Dolls of meat — with feet & hair

*From a Letter to Jack:*

Kruschev's mouth in Kennedy's forehead.

Old Synagogues with mantric shouting & rocking by Hasid-
ic choirs making the room electric on Sabbath Night, religious
orgones streaming from their beards.

Silent coral cities with purple green fish in the wavy blue
waters.

India flowing past the train window with huge plains & palm
trees & cows & people shitting in the grasses & washing with
loincloths in muddy rivers & waterbuffalos & the Ghats mts
in the heat haze way off.

Ganeshes for Peters, Buddhas for the Jacks, Kalis & Durgas
for Bill & ilk — a huge cartoon religion with Disney gods with
3 heads & 6 arms killing buffalodemons.

Imagine my father wandering around New Jersey in orange
robes with big serious expression.

Rishikesh — walking along path near house, three half
naked men sitting with fixed eyes & beards crosslegged all
afternoon in trance under tree — one with a pet cow with a
monstrous deformed jaw his friend — & tin beg cups on the
deerskin mat — fixed bloodshot staring open eyes on one, and
Shiva Tridents stuck into the ground beside them.

Climbed hill & talked to beautiful Jerry Heiserman clear-
skinned long-hair-like-girl shining-eyes youth who just come
down from Himalayas for Spring, sitting on swing, with Rishikesh panorama below his back, in long orange Brahmachari
robes, invited us to Astral lunch.

The sitting bloodshot-eye yogis down below on the path —?
"Ah they're just poster advertisements for the real holy yogis
invisible in the mountains near Gangotri."

Hardwar Kumbh Mela — I saw processions of hundreds of

stark naked ash-smeared saddhus (nagas or snakes) some beautiful kids with long matted hair & other old Breughel bellies & brown Indian balls & hair all over ass & some one legged naked yogis —

one little guy sitting on wall had thin infantile paralysis spider legs crisscrossed in Padmasan position — with tin cup & smile — hair piled around on his head like Shiva's Mt. Kailash, tied with red rag. —

Riding elephants & horses, and all the lady & gentlemen merchants & householders showering their path with flowers — one naked naga under a tree who lives in Hardwar all year under that tree — got up with big belly standing legs apart & blew his conch horn triumphant to see his brothers pass in review to the Ganges along the main street —

Followed by bands of weeping singing homeless women walking along holding on to each other, with no hair & bald like holy humble Gertrude Stein suffering phantoms, actually they made one cry, all dressed in orange robes & singing Sanskrit hymns to Nirvana

So we watched them crowd down the steps to the river & bathe, one old fat bearded naked leader-saddhu first, & then go in dripping and bobbing hundreds washing the ashes off themselves — & then go back up thru streets to the temple where they rang bells & smeared themselves with white ashes all over again —

Elora — Glory, I mean they got great dancing Shivas balanced with ten arms doing cosmic dances of creation 20 feet tall, & fantastic skully Kalis invoking nightmare murders in another yuga, thousands of statues dancing all over huge temple built like Mt. Kailash the Himalayan abode of Shiva — And Ganesha with fat belly & elephant head & snakehead belt & trunk in a bowlful of sweets riding on his Vehicle a mouse — How can Da Vinci beat an elephant on a mouse? —

Two musicians — sit on stage or in a room & the string man begins tweedling meditatively on his raga notes, & then they play not for 15 minutes like on records but 50, 60, 70 choruses *every time* hours on end sometimes, chasing each other à la purest improvized jazz with all the spontaneous comedy of that until they're in a telepathic trance & leading each other back & forth across the floors of flowers of non-music — and they *go on*, so that a concert of 2 or 3 ragas can start at 9 in the evening & they'll play till midnight & if they feel good with full dress audience they go on till dawn.

And Indian singing is something else, a guy sits down surrounded — they all play sitting down barefoot anyway in pyjamas — everybody, workers, walk around in streets in underwear regular striped hollywood nightmare shorts with open flies like Americans have nightmares being caught in the streets in — so the singer sits down & begins groaning and stretches his hand out to catch the groan & whirls it above his head, any noise that comes into his throat like a butterfly, and throws it away with his left hand and catches another hypnotic gesture note with his right hand and whirls it around, his voice follows wierdly way up into high icky giggle gargle sounds and brings it down like Jerry Colonna and stirs it around with his forefinger like its all jello and throws it away with a piercing little falsetto into the curtain and does this over & over again till he's shaking like an epileptic fit and his fingers are flying all over trying to catch the myriad little sounds coming in his ears like butterflies, I said that, like I mean flies well mosquitos, little eees and zoops & eyerolling wheeps! Very much like ipskiddy Yikkle song on your (J.K.'s) tape, but further out delicately lasting for hours and ending back on the original groaning eternity oom, low blues.

Also great dancing makes Barrault seem amateur, it took thousands of years to prepare a perfect wink, Tandava & Nataraja Cosmic dances of Creation & Destruction & Kali dances & hands fluttering in front of male-female god faces & a wierd form of super-tapdancing barefoot where I saw a man *flying* across the stage with his body rigid straight up & his feet fluttering flat on the ground like pogo sticks a dozen times a second, improvising to frantic tabla tatoos — Fred Astaire be amazed in his grey age — so would you you old bore —

Dukkha means not suffering but unsatisfactoryness — So I

heard this stockbroker in pyjamas repeating thrice with impatient sad & angry voice "Dukkha Dukkha Dukkha" like saying trouble trouble trouble annoyed at the light bill, or money money money, existence is always asking me for money.

Houses full of hermaphrodites and further down the block a bunch of cots on the pavement where middle aged transvestites sit & put on rouge, with bald spots on their heads, & comb their long black hair down to the waist & cop on the corner sits in his box & guards everybody from harm. — Bombay Scene

*Oct. 20, 1962 Sat —*

With Peter & Hope Savage, under Howrah Bridge — In Saddhu's hut awhile, smoking & singing — then walked under bridge to hear the cyclonic steel roar — "It's a great machinery" — said the saddhu — speaking of the Universe — then to Nimtallah burning ghat — Many corpses in the noontime flame, one with head all burnt black down to the skull & teeth showing & eyes popped & white — Golgotha resting in place at the head of the woodpile — later, another face all exploded & dripping with fat — later passed by it & the skull had opened, the facebone mask all black slid down where the neck would've been, among charred & burning wood chips — but the brain suddenly revealed — not yet burnt, like a mud river map seen from an airplane, a flow of Conscious mud — the inside cauliflower pudding of the brain yellow-brown in the smoke, slowly turning black & beginning to smoke & soon I saw a burning brain encased in the back of the skull, opened like a powder box. Face mask off like a round box lid, & the riverbed of brain dry brown below, like from an airplane. Looked Majestic.

Or. What's Cooking at the Burning Ghats. Went back tonite (Sat) with Sandeepan & Shakti — sat & smoked pipe with dark skinned older authoritative Saddhu — offered him a Cigarette later, he gave it back "I already have a bidi burning, you're a minute too late" — I answered "I'll save it for the next kalpa" — He thought & thought & replied "Whatever you get from my blessing, paper they call money, Shankar (Siva), Moksha —

keep half and send half to me." I picked up a pinch of burning ground dirt & placed it on my tongue & offered him a pinch. He repeated his request.

Walking out, a family sitting round a woman's corpse on a charpoy loaded with flowers, the bald son caressing the stern face of his mother, eyes & lips closed silent & set & grim as he leaned over her, passing his palm over her forehead & weeping —then rubbed his eyes & suddenly lifted his wrist to glance at his watch. All against the grim red stone concrete wall of the Ghat, next to an ash pit 6 feet long — pillars of the small Rembrandt dream — walling the opposite side. Like a miniature of the ball court at Chichen Itza.

Taxi across Howrah bridge & ate in Mohamedan country liquor house — child sleeping on wet area of footpath — next to scattered broken clay pots & leaves — and a thin small woman carrying brass pot filled with white & yellow flowers, and a one stringed begging-bowl-gopi-lyre combined — and a picture of her guru hung standing before her breast — eyes

squinted, passing by a flower seller. "I never open my eyes on human beings" — Sang plaintive wowl-note indic thin song voice, sad with her face lifted to the streetlight — Baul wanderer, went off singing & twanging as she walked toward the streetcorner lights away from the bridge. "Gopal is my hero . . . Krishna is all I see"

*Oct 20, 1962* Amjadia Hotel Peter asleep me on Ganja 11:30 PM, beggar singing Allah.

Today Oct 20 — Walking around Victoria Memorial — a huge piled cloud big as Calcutta's buildings all in one floating castle — reflected in the dark pool waters — the Tank in the Park, and huge wide lawns to the skyline — in Chinese restaurant the setting sun orange on the wall behind Peter's table & him sitting there looking out silent in the cave — The King of Kings on a vast screen — sudden ken in the dark theater that the message was hypnosis on the Mount — "love your enemies" — "love the State" — "Don't revolt against the world" — badly spoken by the bramachari hollywood blond boy with sensitive chin and light blue eyes — that stared woodenly, as his voice was wooden, with organs and outstretched arms to the red capped crowds on the hillside. Home — Asoke & Raja Yoga talk — in bed. Behala #34 last tram at 11:15 moving away grinding like a giant caterpillar.

"Allen wakes up out of dream bed & says to me:
    Ocean somewhere swimming — I had these tiny blue
    pants on — very far in shallow water — we, (Peter) came
    to huge building in sea with long corridor & window cur-
    tains — corridor 3 blocks long — we realize nobody
    about — we hold eachother arm around armnarm
    around head & legs intertwined — 000 someone comes —
    he goes — we hold closer & decide to screw — I peter grab
    Allen & take his pants down — Allen wakes up &
    says to me "all because of this — Hello — I just
    woke up" & he come over to top me body &
    hugs to play with me." — Note by P.O.

* * *

Damema (Selflessness) is the name of Hevajra's partner at the center of the mandala.

* * *

Byom Byom Mahadeva! (Bom Bom Mahadeo!)　(Invocation to Shiva before smoking Ganja.) Deva of Devas Lord Shiva　Sound of Tandava.
        Similar verse awkwardly transcribed in burning ghat:
    Lata patra tatva jitil vale
    Ba bam bam　ba bam bam　maha sabda gale

# Reading

*Greece: 1961*

Iliad & Oddessy; Guide Bleu to Greece; Cafavy, Sikilianos, Anthologies of Greek Poetry; Archeological Guides; Knossos, Mycenae, Athens etc.; Henry Miller — Colossus of Marroussi. *Israel:* Archaeology of Israel: Penguin; Zev etc. Guide to Israel; Gershom Sholem — Trends in Jewish Mysticism; Mss. of contemporary poetry in translation; Breasted — History of Ancient World; Book on Crusades. Hitti's *Arabs* on Crusades; Cambridge Medieval History on Crusades.
*Ship:* Islands of Spice (Zanzibar); also Zanzibar School History; Mysticism Sacred & Profane — Zaehner; Hinduism — Penguin Series — K.M. Sen; Intro to India — Moraes & Stevenson; Train to Pakistan — Kushwant Singh; Childhood's End — Arthur Clarke; Swahili Aphorisms; Hitler's Table Conversations (Boermann).
*SS Amra Feb.:* Saint on the March — (Vinoba Bhave) — Hallam Tennyson; The Ambassadors — Henry James (finally read thru); Pelican History of Indian Art — Hindu Jain Buddhist. Short History of India & Pakistan; History of India — Chatterjee; Jataka Tales.
*Jan 1, 1962:* Stories from Bengal — Ed. Dr. S. Dutt; Treasury of Asian Lit — Ed. Yohannan (Indian Section); Passage to India — E.M. Forster; Kim — Rudyard Kipling; The Voice of God (Stories) — Kushwant Singh; Waiting for Mahatma — R.K. Narayan; An Autobiography — M.K. Gandhi.
*May 1962:* B. Bromage — Tibetan Yoga; Theos Bernard — Land of Thousand and Buddhas; Persian Miniatures — Faber & Faber; The Religions of Tibet — Helmut Hoffman.
Buddhist Himalaya — David Snellgrove; Foundations of Tib. Mysticism — Lama Govinda; Tibetan book of Great Liberation — Padmasambava: Evans-Wenz; Admiral Doenetz — Memoirs; Theory & Practice of Hell — Kogen (Concentration Camps).
*June:* Tibetan Interviews — Anna Louise Strong; Raise High

71

the Banner of Mao Ze Tung's Thought on Art & Literature — ;
Tibet Fights for Freedom (White Book) India 1960; Homage to
Clio — W.H. Auden; Mao Tze Tung — 19 Poems; The Rape of
Tibet — Nikkil Mantra (Pamphlet Calcutta 1960); On the Hima-
layan Front — Dr. Satyanaryan Calcutta 1960.

*July Sept:* Nagarjuna Chap 1-4; Gertrude Stein — Selected
Works (in and out); Sashibushan Das Gupta — Obscure Reli-
gious Cults; Remakrishna — Gospel (Conversations); Sri
Thakur — Discourses; Red Cats — Anselm Hollo; 2'nd Ave —
Ohara; Like I Say — Whalen; "Indian Thought" pamphlet —
Samaren Roy; The Screen — I A Richards.

*Bombay:* Verses from Shankara; 2 books on Ramana Maharshi;
In and out Histories of Sanskrit Literature; Mudgala Purana;
Legends Myths of India — P. Thomas; Shivananda — Raja
Yoga.

# THE PRIVILEGED CLASS

*(Calcutta) Statesman*

## Bulk Of Wealth Owned By 1% In India

1962

### From Our Special Representative

NEW DELHI, Oct. 23.—Although Prof. P. C. Mahalanobis, who presides over the committee on the distribution of national income, is still engaged in writing the committee's eagerly-awaited report, an authoritative indication is now available of the committee's crucial conclusions.

By far the most important, if depressing, conclusion of the committee is that under the existing state of affairs there is little scope for a diminution of concentration of wealth and economic power in the hands of a few persons.

For this gloomy forecast the committee gives two basic reasons. First the rigorous import restrictions which make the Indian market the most protected in the world, and in which almost anything can be sold at almost any price.

Secondly, the committee feels that the constitutional provision for compulsory payment of adequate compensation for private property acquired by the State would make it extremely difficult to reduce the concentration of wealth.

To press home this point, the committte has analysed in detail the ownership of stock and shares, which form one of the important sectors of private wealth and confer on their owners great economic power.

After painstaking research, based on income-tax returns, the committea has come to the conclusion that 1% of the country's households own as much as 75% of privately-held stocks.

### HIGHLY CONCENTRATED

This is not unexpected. But the really staggering revelation of the committee is that even within this small minority the further distribution of ownership is highly concentrated

More than half the privately-owned share capital in India, the committee underlines, is owned by only 14.000 houses.

In other words, it is only 1% of India's privileged class—which in turn is 1% of the total population—that really owns and controls the bulk of the nation's wealth.

Even that is not the end of the matter. The committee conclusively shows that the "management control" of industries is incredibly more concentrated than "ownership control". With comparatively small share-holding, individuals or business houses are able to take complete charge of the policies and operations of the companies.

### PARADOXICAL FACT

In this connexion, the committee has drawn attention to a paradoxical fact The greater the dispersal of a company's shares, the smaller is the size of the concentrated shareholding required to obtain and maintain control of the business.

In the committee's opinion, the liberal loans by banks and other financial institutions have fostered the trend towards concentration.

*Wednesday, October 24, 1962 Evening*

Revolt of Machines — weapons systems enforce attitudes, Radio
TV teleprint enforce style of speech & statements, economy
enforce living habits etc — Cut up today Kennedy & Tass statements on Cuba Crisis Blockade & the impersonal chatter of diplo-
matic newspaperese sounded like metallo-mechano-averages
computer of marketable ideas proceeding from Nowhere, like
a space ship telepathy station hovering over earth, invisible,
manned by science fiction aluminum-diamond attendants, re-
mote control a la Burroughs "Trust of giant insects from another
galaxy."

*Morning dream*

in a play — in seats in the audience, with friends talking to
Burroughs. They've made a play of Naked Lunch — he's in chair
with long hair — I had visited beat night club earlier once when
it was crowded — someone wrote in newspaper that show was
N.G. When I go back same owner-Commedian is playing to
empty house — complains of no business — his art is uninter-
esting & fake —
    Anyway, Burroughs is there back from America — he has
long hair, blonde-red, looks like Brian Gysin or the con-man
from Texas jail-Paris — I look at him & his face keeps changing, he looks like a big successful spoiled beatnick kid with hair
down to shoulders — says he saw play version of his book in
NY when he was there — I ask how it was — "Oh, well, you
know — not bad, there were really some very good sequences
that got the point across — the actors, etc" — I realize it isn't
Burroughs & say so to Jack next to me who says "Don't be silly
he just has a different hair-cut" — I stare at Burroughs down
the row of seats & he averts gaze & stares back, finally I ask him
who he is, "Well, I suppose I'm Burroughs" — "No you're not,"
I insist — his face clarifies & looks less & less Burroughs-
familiar & more like a grown up Jerry Heiserman. It's *not*
Burroughs.

Selection of Kerouac's *Mexico City Blues* for Penguin, my choices:
Choruses # 13, 17, 24, 50, 51, 52, 54, 63, 64, 96, 97, 110, 113, 121, 137, 146, 149, 155, 173, 179, 182, 199, 202, 208, 209, 211, 217, 219, 225, 228, 230, 232, 239, 240, 241-42.

*November 3 '62*

Walking up Central Avenue — the sudden crash of Trams on rails, hoot of auto horns in the early evening dark, buses roaring from exploding motors, clank of rikshaw bells, cries of brakes of cars, voices in the rush hour streets — later a murky darkness in the streets as a trolley with yellow eyes crawled thru the smog on Chitpur bend.

Hours with Sunil Ganguli, Shankar Chatterjee drunk, Moti Nandy, in blue shirt, Sandepan across the coffeehouse table, a cold coffee, Shakti Chattergee coming later — Shankar yelling & vomiting in the W.C. — & walk into Moslem section near the Mosque. Seeing Asoke Fakir catch the bus to Bowhanipore.

\* \* \*

KHEER

An ounce of yellow colloidal milk
            sweet in my mouth
Fans whirling, green neon light,
A man in a turban and french beard
under the electric switch, an auto horn
and the Street, rolling with
            the clang of Trams:
What a white small lady beggar with
            her hand in the car window —
Grey beards & basket carriers passing
            in Silhouette —
A bus roars by with people
            in pants hanging out the doors
The great scratch-cough of

75

        strangle throat
    cigarette eaters spitting
        in the hand wash sink.
                    Bentick St. Calcutta
                    Winter 1962

*Nov 7 —*

Last nite Tues (puja) nite at Nimtallah Burning Ghat — a few
black skulls in the woodpile — Pouring white fat (ghee) into the
flames, it burns brighter and sparks shoot out, the body burns
faster — an old man wrapped in white carried in on a wood
woven-string couch — thin caved-cheek bony forehead — and
a little girl lying on the woodpile, her mother wrapped in white
collapsed, singing a psalm, on the ground nearby.

Over the wall in the gathering ground of ganja saddhus, a
huge midnight circle, many crosslegged men with pipes, cymbals clanging, a drum, and two men dressed in women's veils
and saris, whirling like dervishes, a few boys in blue shirts
whirling against them — occasionaly rhythmic shuddering of
the hips, and crawling crab-legged on the ground pumping
pelvis back & forth between different circles of devotees under
different trees — all joining in waves and diminishing separately again — Sat down with a saddhu in orange robes and puffed
his pipe.

*Nov 13-14 —*

Night at the burning ghat — 25NP 2 triangle paper packets of
ganja — at the main st. pipe shop — Long haired scruffy orange
robe saddhu with thin nose & long droopy hip face, chattering
animatedly in broken English — from Gauhati, his ashram —
we go there? — Benares? — Pranayam — in main Ganges St.,
the cymbal chorus in the brick shed — "men from Bihar" —
chain-cymbals clashing & chanting all nite — A body burning in
the first ash pit — pile of wood & the head slowly bubbling up
around mouth and nose — Cheeks blackened with sheets of

flame clasping the volume of the face — splitting, and pink underskin sizzling open — Sat on the bench & watched five minutes, staring at the head — feet painted red sticking out the other end of the wood structure bed —

In the Mandir, the handsome naked torso yogi with big strong face, and red bushy-curled hair — sitting with red robed black faced beard with little eyes who exchanged amicable glance, full eyed stare — my strained back against the (concrete) marble door post — sharing a pipe I coughed & so began roll my own cigarette — First saddhu friend appeared & continued grinding the brown bagleaf in palm with his thumb, wet drops & tobacco mixed to almost damp paste — I rolled in cigarette — away again after long sit, & prasad — salute to the handsome Saddhu who made his chest glisten with oil & muscular shining breasts & happy smile — he rubbed down a thin saddhu's belly — and beamed with joy when in return, a hand passed round & round his chest from nipple to nipple rubbing in the heated oil — burned a pan of ghee, & one pea prasad for ceremony — then lay down to sleep on a piece of white thin cloth in the corner — "You're beautiful man" I said to him thru first thin nose Saddhu — he brought out a big handful of Prasad — smiled like child at me — "Healthy he smoke all day people come sit down make him smoke smoke all day all night — he just sleep an hour — lay down head with all that in it" — I lay & snoozed next to him awhile, sleepy Darshan — then walked out for tea, gave bhoog (prasad food) — bought tea & leaf of patties & potato curry, for the other loony saddhu I seen dance jazzy burlesk at Kirtan — he smiled too — boy next to him stole his cigarettes from table — "It ate it" & gave him another — all ash smeared & a hump-backed rump at base of his spine under the dusty tantric red loincloth. and a white worn spread over his shoulder — back to the ghats from tea — sat at fire by old Babu with Kailash-pile of hair on his head who slept greyly on his side —

coming away an old ashy grey fellow followed me for an anna — I said no, irritably — touched his feet — he begged — I touched his feet he reached for mine & I slipped away — returning from 2:30 last chant crisis of Bihari boys — he squatting

77

alone on step of sleeping mandir, chanting Ram Hari Bol song
alone in froggy beautiful lone voice — long long, as I passed I
placed 25NP at his feet & he reached out & touched my foot —
I lay down awhile alongside handsome Saddhu's corner, near his
charcoal brazier — still glowing with a new chunk taken from
the burning pits — But the Priests came & sloshed water &
opened the gates & turned on lites so I left & went wandering the
burning pits again — Now all groups resolved, silent & grey,
crazy & suave together around several pit fires they cared for
warmth — one halfnaked saddhu stretched with his loincloth
slipped off his buttock looking like one of the dead corpses beside
the all nite fire of the old man whose head I saw adorn the pile
earlier that even, now all ash in the ganges spreading out near
the steps on the brown muddy surface like inkstain mushroom
— a few kids at another fire with old gentle round faced bald
saffron Pop. And my singing beggar now squatting on a red pit,
lucidly chanting away gods name — I thought perhaps this be
Master Sign since I been earlier so rejectful to him & he turning
out to be such a simple holy sustained all nite praying fellow like
this in front of my eyes — I sat on bench near his fire & he talked
to me in loud voice, a speech I couldn't follow, sounded like he
complaining my being so selfish waving his arms at me from his
little brushwood hot flamey pile — I moved away, just in case he
get further noisy or mad — finally to sleep after another pipe at
the handsome Saddhu's side in the Mandir — a strange & simple
orange robe squatted by & made me & him and another attendant
a pipe. I blasted enough till my throat dry & panicky — then
walked up & down my body trembling my neck constricted till
I peed, & still the trembling wait, as if I vomit or Ramakrishna
appear in the river — or Krishna in every animal eye all around,
each of the beggars — lay down to sleep finally on marble bench
in inner waiting room with rows of Baul singers and rags saddhu
buttocks sheeted on the floor — left my rubber sandles below —
when I awoke, — I had drifted to sleep earlier as nites before on
ganja seeing a sort of crystal cabinet Krishna beribboned &
jeweled in minds eye — thru universes of feet & skulls & fire
& wars and firesides — crystal cabinets a-million — found my

footrubbers disappered from their place on the floor. Walked out glanced around each old spot of the night — where the ash pit men were smearing their morning skin — I had wakened, thinking it all a cartoon dream, no longer trembling, as the temple bell-gong shout rose to a noisy Bong climax like the end of a laughing gas movie — shoes gone like Donald Owl — went barefoot for tea & puris & potatos. Tram Car 19 home all the way to Dharmatalla 8 A M.

*Nov. 1966*

Fuck Kali
   Fuck all Hindu Goddesses
   Because they are all prostitutes
     *[I like to Fuck]*
          All Hindu Goddesses
            are Prostitutes
     Fuck Ma Kali
   Mary is not a prostitute because
     she was a virgin
   Christians don't
   Worship prostitutes
     like the Hindus
          Fuck ma Kali
Fuck          Fuck all Hindu Goddesses
Kali         Because they are all prostitutes
Durga
Laxmi
     I like to Fuck all Hindu Goddesses

*Nov-Dec 1962 — Train to North Bengal*

The half-horizon moving green fields of Paddy, with an island oasis of light brown earth & bushes — palmtrees standing toothpick leafy sphinx — and a mile far back, with red tower and drifters of smoke in the clear air beneath a great roof of smoky clouds broken by blue light sky as the — Car grinds to a halt at the aluminum iron fence thru which black mother pig & four smaller climbed up a gully to the path by thatchroof, — Tree and red dummy square smoke-stack was passed by a flock of birds, and the cow swished its tail cropping the grass — and a brick wall had a crack in the outhouse Criscross opening. Peter in green shirt long hair curling on the shoulder in the light smokey Junction light — and a bush sprung with orange flowers — and the men's & women's voices discussing the murmur of the (voyage). Silence in the long brown bench in the railroad wooden afternoon — just time near for the trip's end, and the passenger train stopped for a lengthening minute — little boy bangs the big door-exit shut and sticks his head out the window.

*Nov-Dec. 1962 —*

*Visit to Tarapith — in Birbuhm area, Bengal, home of 19th Century holy fool Bama Kape.*

In yellow oil-lamp-light under the thatched porch, crosslegged on burlap mat, the orange-robed saddhu, long black hair, hollow cheeks, and eyes gleaming squatting in his door — inside a small altar & raised bed, incense before Kali's image photo — the lamplight flicker, Shakti Chattertee Poet explains how he was dead walking on the road — When he took his last puff got up & start walking, everybody everything blackened — his body we have burnt in the burning ghat — he shouted & cryed — some white thing, holding some whiteness & walking with the whiteness, at his side — Just an hour ago.

Cries of Hari Bol! Jai Tara! from the woods — the twinge of locusts in trees — as before dim beep of firefly light flying dotting the trees with the blinking stars — Shakespearean Ardens and I said "Did you think you were a fly on the (mirror) looking glass of the moon?" —

Walking on pitch moonless night a mile on country path from the fair — where ate sweets and heard a trio of drums held like barrels against the chest in the courtyard before the image of Kali dancing — Mahamaya's dream on Shiva's breast, her foot & tongue stuck out & black face & white eyeballs painted on the flat stone face — Dancing with drum one boy before me — then sat on a hill with several, in the shit complained Ashok — and passed a pipe — You must write when you're dead — "Give consciousness to the mind which will write — One mind in the burning ghat, one walking in death & one watching & writing —" "As I'm not dead I can smoke again," replies Shakti.

81

Fireflys blinking in the trees — Victory to Ramakrishna. Victory to Chaitanya! Victory to Gaurenga! Victory to Ram! Victory to — many people singing Hari Bol Hare Hare Krishna Krishna in the night in the woods — Now in the lamplight, the pipe goes around — A mosquito-net bedecking his bed in the Cubicle — Boom Boom Mahamaya! ! ! ! A smell without a Guru says Ashok . . . "If I really going to die this time" says Shakti — "Yes the cellular network is different in each brain, no different Universe but the experience is of mind-stuff, Citta, and everyone experiences that" — "Why don't you experience death more and more?" — Scented pipe, Peter "smoking like a chimney" slow silent puffs — "Yeah" — his voice breaking in answer — and an answering voice in the gloom — a voice chanting alone, the headmaster of his school — "What time is it now, Puja time?" —' 'He's an Asura." — Mosquitos on my wet-pajame'd knee — flitting on the page — Is it against the dharma to kill mosquitos? — bacteria eating amoebas — Last night, the lamb, which had been trembling, tied to a pole in the temple enclosure before Kali's image — wet head, its little bah almost inaudible in the thump-boom of drums playing music to the Jai Citaram death — that lamb help held upsidedown its head in the chopping prongs, while young man in white cloth swacked the big sharp scythe down silently & the head fell off — the body pushed into a line of watching girl childs who scattered — lay on the floor stunned & suddenly waved a foot, a foot and wriggled & tried to walk on the air, kneeled to rise & stepped over wriggling its muscles to walk — the foot the leg lamb waving under the eye — furred and small, headless beast.

"When again & again the world will be covered with vice & sin I will come to bring peace to the people in vice & sin — I shall come to Establish Religion — I shall be possible in every age — / In this life you are the almighty god / wherever you put me" — a walking seed, with legs on the wall of the mud — insect crept along the floor under my foot's shadow — Ashok in orange cloth in middle, yellow Peter Shirt — My beard & red nightgown — "Shakti, get up — you will go high, but you will not die" — a Perfumed cigarette — Anandamai!

82

Went back the next morn to the woman faced Saddhu's hut —
the story of Saint Bama Kape — set fire to house & ran away
— made Kali image of cowdung — banged tin pans — at age
65 went to Kalighat — Court closed & all Puja arrangement
made before Kali — Bama Kape smoked & drank — The Ganja
Mudra — As the red pipe passed round on the burlap pack —
leaning against a charpoy for backrest, that had been hung from
the roof, against Bamboo poles — Joined by Moslem Fakir who
in Purple lungi & white torn shirt says "My heart is a prince &
mouth advocate" —
    "If you worship Bama Kape you'll get everything" — Sings
prayer for the poor — drums beating, 10 AM at the temple —
"Who awakes Bama gives power to awake him who awakes
Bam" — Asoke translating every few sentences — then big
Bengali discussions of the cigarette & chopping block for ganja
& the metal chopper — with pointed hook handle for poking &
cleaning pipe — the Silent host in long washed-out nylon
orange robes — Young girls on road & child in arms crying at
a family of monkies on the road watching them — all making
noise at silent Monkeys waiting for a handout — "Why don't
you say what you mean" — "If you don't know anything you'll
be like a goat —"
    At dusk, a long sunset walk through paddy fields into the
dark, arriving at a Saddhu's bright lamp, & porch — saw his
blue image of Kali with delicately painted eyes, where he sat,
"Ask him any question" — in Saffron robe and long black hair,
said he was 89 years old — Swami Shivananda Hamsa Puri —
"Breathe air into your mouth" — as in smoking ganja — "deep
into the lungs & fill out the belly — hold it there & expell thru
one or another nostril" — That being the first step of prana-
yama — as sitting on the temple porch at Tarapith earlier, high
on some ganja for the fourth lovely continuous day — surrounded by bells and trees and naked green fields to bathe in the brown
river — now leaving Tarapith to the rr stop — now sitting on
the marble bench in lamplight, with sleepers shrouded around

under the high single dim station light in its huge glass cap —
Shakti sitting on the floor in nought but shirt & bare legs —
singing grounded Tagore — Peter rolling more cigarettes —
waiting for the 10:45 train to go to Suri.

All morning again in the porch — when a drunken Saddhu
came roaring up & dragged me into the bushes & put his Brah-
man string around my neck — "Come to me alone and I'll show
you Tara Ma" — but Tara took us away at dusk — he had stag-
gered up the road to the shacks of Tarapith with his tall bald-
shaven companion in cups, who kneeled at everyone's feet in
orange loin diaper & had big rosaries and a top-knot pigtail on
his shaven skull — thin belly, who twisted himself up drunken-
ly to kiss each one's feet — Now Asoke Fakir singing softly in
the Railroad Station calm — and the woman with the strong
face also in sunyassini safron with loud voice "Jai Guru" to
whom I gave tea twice, and a rupee & piece of sugar candy sweet
prasad — God food offerings — as we left her standing on the
dusty road under a tree near Bama Kape's shrine's statue — he
sitting naked in pink Marble with a fox & snake companion —
thru the barred window his flesh-colored statue almost moved
like a 3-D photograph —

And sitting in the grass behind the compound of the ganja-
country-likker shop (smelling like alcohol & dip your finger in,
to the candle, watch the blue flame halo the hotty finger) — the
young longbearded Swami with umbrella kid attendant who
oiled his hair & massaged his feet — "Japa Krishna Nam" singing old Asoke sweetly — "Japa Rama Krishna" — rising to
silent light notes, wavering in the gloom — the Indian sleepers
having now sat up to watch us sit & smoke & sing —

The long story of an old saint beginning from Mahabharat's
Kunti cursing a temple because no food for the Pandavas too
late at night — 1880 or 1860 Saint came & dug up the Ancient
Mandir, prophesied a baby for the Maharaja of Kashmir — he
who ate of the leavings of the Fox — fed the poor, died — the
temple fell in and the Maharaja sent no more — told us by Saddhu who now living there invited us by his story, got up & said,
I am going back — as we headed in the opposite direction —

toward the night dark paddy fields & the Railroad.

And Bama Kape himself, as described by the old white-haired pandit beard who gave us a room — eating the prasad in his own Kali mouth & surrounding his head with tara flowers — drinking and beaten up & smoking ganja with the Saddhus who passed thru Tarapith till he — since he a young man sent from home as child — crazy woman Saint — big lush, Sirs, everybody thought he was crazy except Ramakrishna who stood under his feet in Kalighat the time Bama Kape came down on a single visit — a big idiot — dwelled on *Tara*.

\* \* \*

On the train — woke up an old man in thin white old muslin shawl who slept on the bench & sat down next to him, finishing another stick of T. Then the train rolling thru darkness — houses concrete walls below in shaft light from Car windows — sleepers on the luggage racks asking the time — I want the joy of Maya, not only the Dukkha — at last Crosslegged on bench my white riverwashed pajamas & deep breaths filling my body till I entered the hole & came out 3 breaths later to see the brown shelves of the car, thinking of the Joy of Maya, that I smelt the first Aether. Pound recommended yoga instead of "drugs" in typewritten note on window of disciple-Rabblerouser skeleton's bookshop — 1950 — Bleecker St. across from the Mills Hotel. It all began in the Mills Hotel — me blowing Jack — and his vision of an old man, at the window of his flophouse cubicle masturbating for hours.

\* \* \*

"Remove those dark SATANIC mills"

— — —

> In a straight fight, hey god
> We shall meet together face to face,
> with secret weapons
> in the meantime I prepare myself
>     & become strong like Veseuvius.
> Tho an Emperor in nerves
>   & blood Corpuscles / yet
>   the family of the defeated grows

I am the *one* of this Hell
             Empire of people (the only Satan)
Yet the taste of Heaven, I remember.
         Now for some more time
     You pass your nights in
         yr garden of Eden with easy relaxed pleasure.
And now with the dancing
         nymphs
             and become buttersoft body
             & become a possessor
                 of the breast nectar
of Uroboshi Ramnagar in
             her dances
     you become butter soft mind
Devastation — impertinence —
         Let the call of the devastating
challenger
             dry up the blood
     and the gut bow string music
             rhythm end —
And by that time O God in my
         day to day middle class bit by bit
             & Poverty I shall
             fight on, fight
and raise my broken head again
     in undaunted Courage.

Weak lisping borning
Because of God life saving
             herb is
                 not in your hand.

O god I shall meet you in
         the depths of the Middle
             Class blood
No!   You are going to be
     defeated, sure.

Your every nerve is filled
    with white ants
in the bones & flesh & marrow
    only to age old
        cripple heritage
        of blood —

God by that time I am a
        master fighter for
    the day's fight
    I have got the eternal right
    of the unachievable
    classical Bow-weapon —
Tho I'm vanished ages ago
    from heaven —
I am that Satan, the firstborn
    child of heaven.

    Poem by Shakti Chatterji,
    Crudely translated, fast oral transcription —
                    * * *
    A Painstaking table & chair & wooden flowers —
Corpses of some sad flowers — one or 2 shady paintings on the
wall — like the invited souls that time has forgiven them —
allowed them to live — at Purna Das' House
                    * * *

BAUL SONG FRAGMENTS

*(Copied thru Asoke Fakir's fast translation, while Purna Das
sang from his aged sick bed paralyzed in a hut in Birbhum.)*

Baul — "No attachment, nothing to do Except Krishna devotion —"

— — —

The hairy hand of darkness playing with my Corpse.

— — —

Been around the Universe 8,000
                times — That 14 cubits of land
If you only plowed it properly
            You could have grown gold.
O Listen mind, pick up the Spade
                of Bhakti-Virtue
& start digging the ground of
        your own body
& destroy the grasses of
        Sin —

                        — — —

O my mad mind you didn't plow
                Your human body
You don't know O mind what
                you have to do.
You have to account for what
            you have done in yr last life
            (to God)
He's the Thakur of 3 Universes who
            knows his last 3 lives —
Why don't you try to remember
            that after 80,000 cycles
            you only got 14 cubits of land.

O my mad mind my mad mind you could
            have plowed & grown gold.
You've really wasted such a
            wonderful land of love
            & you didn't grow anything —
When the Call will Come,
        No excuses no protection
        No one will stop Him from
                taking you away —
O listen my mind!   Hold the
            Spade of devotion! —
and remove all the grass of sin —
Take up the Mahamantra

88

            given by the Great Guru,
& sow the seed.

There are 6 persons with you
            They eat yours, & take everything
                        from you, you don't
            know what evil they
                        do you —
Leave them & Catch Sri Gaurenga,
offer prayers to the heart of Chaitanya.
                — — —
Don't stop the desire of Radha
& end hunger of mind for
                        Waves of "Nectar" —
in this body I have all my pleasures
            and joys —
O blue dressed woman why don't
            you put on your blue dress again
Put vermillion on yr forehead
            & come before me as a lover,
& wind & bind & plait my hairs —
plait my hair in the style of a lover
anybody — you become Purush and
            I become the man (Prakrit)
You cover your face & turn like an
            angry love lady —
I came to play the flute in Brindiban
Now I give the flute to you,
            young girl —
What my flute says now, sometimes
            say Krishna & Radha —
            Why don't you take my flute
            & let it sing on yr lips
            Raddha Radha Radha —
Neiloconto says — I am the
                        thirst of thirsties —
            great thirstiest thirst.   I am thirsty

                        89

       for great thirst — for the form —
   my Roop of Radha.
Dash — If even I can remove
   my Das & become Dasi (fem)
   I hope I can see the Roop of Radha
I know Radha will give me my
                    blessings
                    — — —

700 women & men
       came from Brindaban,
pissed in Jamuna — rose overflowing
       in waves, the villagers
rushed to see what — "Please stop
pissing and we'll feed you."
          Same at Navadip, the villagers
saw all the water rushing & put
on their clothes around their heads & prayed
please stop pissing & we'll feed you.
                    — — —

The tree & tree joined roots at the stem
       and are bearing fruit there —
Waves of flowers & fruits a going on out,
O Mind listen I shall tell you
You have drowned me
You become greedy for others' wealth,
How long can you eat that?

The tree is in deep waters
       and the branches come out from
              the root which is in Hell.
                 And if you see that you
                 become mad —
Gods name has no like image.
Gods name is no form,
It has no form like image.
Where can you find him
       Who is born without Seed — ?

          Baul Riddle: —
There is one child in 3 wombs (at a time)
The child speaks out his heart to everybody
          but doesn't speak to me —
                    — — —
The light-man comes & speaks
          of light
in the morning walks on 4 paws
and at midday the cat walks
          on 2 feet
and third part of the day
          cat walks on 3 legs &
                    goes back home.
And calamity happens
          near the Ganges —
They kill the Brahmins & go
          live in heaven —

Mss. in Suri, belonging to Purna Das
          *Madan Bhasma*
          Composed & Sung by Krishnachandra Das Goswami
in year 1306.
          This was completed as of Kartik 1306
                    * * *


          SHANTINIKETAN

     Abode of Pearl!   the half
          Moon!   Mosquitos
          at the ankle
     The acrid grey pain of
          too much tea in the
          stomach —
     Paranoic girls averting
          their eyes under the
          trees

                    91

sitting with long hair
   under 1896
      blossoms
Here is the department
   of This & That
Here is no place
   to sleep us
   no place to eat
No professors to talk
   to about moonlit
   American Messengers
Nagarjuna's ghost voice
   talks out of the Zero
   of a new mouth
   in the tea shop next
   to the agro economist
— They don't know which
   way to go off the
      stage
And they all walk
   around thinking
   about Father
      Tagore —
How he would hate those
   thin nosed girls
How he would grieve
   over these professors
   with bad teeth
How he wd. pity these
   Poor students full
   of curried potatos
   and uneducable —
Rid!   No new Books
   in the library!
They say the poems
   in singsong Bengali!
The girls don't talk!

The boys don't make love!
Only the Siamese philosopher
    with the delicate
        porcelain head
Giggles upSide down
    by the library door
    in Sunyata
and steals my pen.

*Notes for Lecture (on New US Prosody to Marxist Literary Conference) Dec 1962*

1) The reason for changes — increased depth of perception on nonverbal-nonconceptual level.
   a) Spontaneous natural visionary
   b) Organized experiment in consciousness:
      1. thru jazz ecstacy & mantras
      2. thru that Electronic machinery
      3. thru drugs
      4. tantra & Zen meditation.

Consequences in poetic composition: an attempt to include more simultaneous perceptions and relate previously unrelated (what were thought irrelevant) occurrences.

   By means of:
1) Reliance on spontaneous writing to capture the whole mind of the Poet — not just what he thinks he should think with his front brain.
2) Interest in the   awkwardness
                     accidents
                     rhythm
      jump of perception from one thing to another breaking
                     syntactical order
                     punctuation order
                     logical orders
                     old narrative order
                     meaning order.

Notations of process of mind

                   & relative natural process
                   Uncensored by
                           grammar
                           syntax
                           order
because these Conventions
           we find not a
           rational, ordering of
                 experience
           but an attempt to
                 censor experience
& keep out certain
           facts which embarrass
& throw doubt on   .
           whole of previously
           accepted
           Human
           Humanistic
           rational
Reality —
                            * * *

J. Sharma — 8 Chandni Chowk, Calcutta
c/o T. Singh
Gent who explains sound. Radha Swami Satsang.
                            * * *
"The Conscious experiencer travels along traces of sound
           (sabdh) to the ultimate vibration."
                                        Traverses the Sound.
                            * * *
"I affirm that Tristan Tzara discovered the word *dada* on the 8th
of February 1916, at 6 o'clock in the evening. I was there with
my 12 children when Tzara pronounced for the first time this
word, which aroused a legitimate enthusiasm in all of us. This
took place at the Cafe de la Terasse in Zurich and I had a roll of
bread up my left nostril." — Jean Arp.   (As recorded by R. H.
Wilenski)
                            * * *

                              94

Tattvārtha Sutra
UMĀSVĀTI
Text:
Jain Sage 7th Century
\* \* \*
God Cathedral of goiters, god
iron boxes enlarging boxes
grandiose comic towering
skeletons of Boxes
God Rocks, structures & turning inside out
Proteins & protozoic waves
of acid electricity —
God growing into scales
& serpent sizes
enlarging in the very
mouth
Red Fangs, god whirling
in the heat
in iron fans under ceiling
Black Clouds piling up
on the coffin lid of
the horizontal wavy
water
Boom Boom Boom in the
engine, iron
Stairways to the Deeps
bulbous heads of brass and
pink one-eyed skin —
Long pheasants tails &
trailing long fins —
Reptile crawling up the
ladder to the moon —
Birds flying inside the
mountain of green
locust-mustache
brown sticks of feces

95

                    descending from
                    aperture in the girley
                        child-buttocks —
out on the streetcorner
                    God pulling rickshaw
                        past to the
green fields by the
                    Fort God's
                        vague stone dwelling —
playing chess with pink
                    boardwalks and
                            sandy beaches,
Sandcastle's beards
                    dropping into the
                        wavelets —
empty pages scrawled
                        with wriggling worm
                    cigaretts disappearing
                            Ink
            smoke              spectre
Post box mouth eating
            angry letters to
                    Bosnia-Herzegovina
dirty books from Ulan
                            Bator
Thumb prints on the
            vast miniature
                    sidewalk —
on the movie Screen —
Double Exposure
Stalin Dreaming in
        the dome-vast
                    obscurity
Eating carrots,
playing with his Cock,
Lounging in Miami Hotel
        in Heaven

in a big Chartreuse
        silk armchair
giving orders to ping pong
        enthusiasts
who are very frightened only
        playing for money
a dollar at a time, what
Chance have they against
the measureless Roubles
        of Death's treasurer —
Sophie Tucker fantasy in
        the streetcar,
having a baby army,
giving in to the luxury

*Nov 12, 1962*
*Kharagpur Train Stop*

The drone of Tea sellers, fried pancake, cold sweets in the cold
black air 11:15 : the long train stretched backward out of nar-
rowing long red cars to the neon shelter under the glowing half
moon blue star points in the sky, the row of yellow station lights,
and a bright box red telegrams accepted here by the lone brick
wall. A dog sniffs the under-irons of the III'd class sleeper coach
— I cough heavily, phlegm burst of stomach gas ganja just
smoked by the side of the Puri train Express — The drone of the
sellers crying repeatedly their poories fried in oil — yodeling of
the end of a grey old throat for water — a regular Thackur music
— Pannay, Pan! — runs the little boy along the train — Conductor with white badge & scarf covered his ears — and in the
train the long corridor of light blanketed sleepers — a long clean
red aisle, blue lights in the roof — Shelves tripled two abreast
in little compartments. The shadow folding its arms on the floor.
Over my shoulder, — sitting by the open door — the great calm
of the sleepers in their wooden racks — contented to sleep in
this roaring space-monster — Soaring along the tracks thru the
Vast — the light of the high lamp whitening the leaf-dark green

97

trees — above an open door in the brick — past which the 2nd old watercarrier slowly wheels his heavy can, bare legs & wool black shoulder — the train whistles & sweatered conductor closed the door — I coughed & went backward to my bunk, with Peter doubled barefoot on the hanging green boards — some paint drip on the aisle side by the iron ladder — make a cosmic splash space-picture — I sniff to see it's real — Time with Governor Greyhair Romney — Pushing him for what For Prexy — Prexie Wexy of Worldy — Indians talking Indian from their shelves — kneeling on the floor is father pushing his dry valise, and climbing back in the covers — I'll go up the ladder & sleep.

All sorts of bunk thoughts eyes closed over the Guru, Swami Satyananda's two thumbs "Be a sweet poet of the Lord" — in the garden on the Ganges — crowded with "devotees," fat bellies seated on the porch after rice on leaf-plates on the house — The big floor, they gave me too much to eat — the mixtures of the universes — O yes the universe without Ether — I mean tho I didn't suffer the tooth-pull pain on Ether, I will when I die perhaps — one may — decompose painfully after a violent space ship crash — bleeding over the cactus-metal door, flesh hanging in chunks of palpitating meat — at least 5 minutes the lamb had of that — Only its head chopped off all at once — & held down with 2 hands by the assistant chopper — strangely — I didn't see it move but he held it down by the mouth still a long time. And kicked the live-rubbery body into a crowd of little girls who ran — which furry white body waved its legs in the air in vain — unable to get right side up — making some kind of noise thru the neck.

*Puri — Nov 13, 1962*

Pot tricks — Peter blows nose & I think it's matches burning in his face. In the teashop off the beach. After swim & walk.

Sunset, sitting crosslegged on the sand bank overlooking the ocean below, waves roar like car crashes — in the blue spread — Orange circle inching below the horizon, green waters, facing my eye, in my head — Smoking & pranayam holding breath

4:16:8 vaguely as the sky colors sharpened and the liquid tip of edge light gold sank, out there so small over the beach buildings & palms and calm sky. (4 inhale 16 hold 8 exhale breath.)

— — —

High clear wind over the gigantic cardboard reflector to white loudspeaker on right: tables of Indians with smooth hair and clean clothes & gentle effeminate Dance gestures: the two mustached boys dancing in front of the noise — and an hour sitting last week in the Underground — a Cellar country liquor shop where Eunuchs dance & boys gather & pat their hair.

— — —

Puri — Dream — back from Europe looking up old girls — Helen Frankenthaler in apartments in N.Y.

Any old girls will do. Long halt. Puri Konerak Bubanishwar. Slight Dysentery. Lunch in the State Guest House. Stall fries — potato chips, sweets, teas,

— high sight of Muckteshvara & Parasumeramahesvera Temples — Shiva's Dance with an erection Nataraja. Can't write much despite the brilliance of the small temples — too much ganja — I can't keep track of my thoughts without effort. What was the fourth thought back? Struggled over that for a day, like remembering dreams — no remember dreams hardly all week or write.

Muleteshvera temple sat on wall & rolled smoke & stared — mediterranean sunlight — on the bright red carved stone — little E.E. Cummings "F"s of stone pinched out like cartoon exclamation points on the "Jagmohan" roof? — The crazy crests like Maya or Aztec helmetry mental formations — fireshapes coming to aesthetic p spade endings — like early drawing doodle I did, Jack of Traces.

Lingams worshipped here. Flowers arranged in the dim Darshan cellarlike light of the inner Sanctum, 10 AM sun rays falling into the well of blot-light — making neon of the little pink & white flower mouths opened shining on the granite black lingams — Attendant intoning Om Shantih inside whilst I sat against checkerboard grill stone outside & listened thru that orient red window in the shade. Heard the music out of the drainpipe near the altar. Then the thickset stone walls of the miniature wheel-temple — looking up the side of the "Deul" tower it rose up to Pevsner infinity in a curve of tractor teeth fading like Iowa into curved blue space with a lotus visible edge stone at the top — giving impression when high of a moving conveyor belt of images & Inca signs & unnoticed small stone scratches & sitters & beasts with trunks on the brick, & perforations for regular design holes — and pretty scenes of seated gods in the center — big bellied Ganesh with his trunk knocked off — the missing jaws & tusks but that big sky belly traversed in a circle by the worldsnake for Brahmin-string — his mousie praying — sweets piled up in the bowl, where his stone trunk moved — big Disney Dumbo feet — I worship Dumbo, the Porpoise.

Somewhere I thought "What if the Universe were in Secret Control of the Whales?" Lots of mistakes though. I saw someone address Peter & interrupted to link the two — but it wasn't happening out of my mind right — the man said "What" — "I say, were you addressing him — I mean did you ask him — " lamely — "Que? Hugh?" — "O nothing I was just dreaming" I said & turned away to his puzzlement & my own —

Up on a platform the great Wheels & Spire of Lingaraj I didn't enter — at early light, at dusk, at night with blue stars over the temple tops — always the silent of the court — a light night burning in the temple — doors shut after 9:30 at the main gate where few but pandas wait — no saddhus as in front of Puri Lion gate P. & I sat & smoked with bearded black saffron robed gentle enquirer — with his head tilted politely aside, & in English spoken "Where are you I beg pray from Sir? You come from" — "America" — "Oh" — retiring — so we sat with him next night & puffed his red clay stovepipe toy — He spread an instant plastic paper seat for us — on the dark ground front of the tall column on which little Garuda bird prays to the sky — by front of Lion Gate I said — gang of cymbal-drum singers Bhajans — Ram Hari Krishna Hari Om! — Circle shirts gathered — smoked and left — for Batia Dharamsala after day at beach & night — I high there crosslegged on sand ledge over ocean sang & prayed aloud to the orange sunset as it fell in the ocean near the western southern should be shore — that long line of beach stretching with a van Gogh boat partycolored bound by rope on beach tilted down to tide — to the burning ghats, a woman saried, carried hanging by arms & knees by several white clothed mourners round the woodpile — then laid on it with black hair, thin, face down, arm folded resting under extended left arm, as in true sleep — the pile wood not big enough — on the inclined beach pitted with ash black spots —

The long beach of Navadip, with log-burned squares — nobody there but dogs walking round at nite to sniff — said there was rotten meat there but no not saw that — Asoke praying meditating alone awhile — I sat on sand & looked at Ganges brown & the design of lights far away looking like signals was it then? or in Calcutta? (Drawing)                                                    the lights ashore.

"Man has no right to be." Just now smoking — 4 thoughts before that? Exactly, try. Me sitting with left leg bare, crossed on lap, one foot to the concrete floor on edge of wood charpoy clothed with sheet, pants folded for pillow & I thought what if he (Louis?) could see me now what case of Dispossession, a flashlight & handkerchief & books by rubber shoes on the ground, Peter been in room all day sleeping in gloomlight smoking many & many cigarettes & ganja in pipe — I brought up sweets & tea & fruits — Sattvic diet — thinking all that 4 thoughts back *Every 3 thought be my grave* — to Cummings, Why? — to literature, with a capital Me. Pound. They never did see India — glad I got here I thought by road, long afternoon walks to New Town Bubaneshwar Market & black fields wandering with Peter into aerodrome barefoot with our new flashlight — flashlight as on Konerak we clomb up in dark & shined lights on girl figures & giant tambourine-drum dancers with big round breasts up high on the roofs of the building with Lotus on top we climbed to — crawling over high stone lotus tower — to rest on top looking at Breughel Blue ocean thru the trees, & red road — we rushed along later at dusk to the long ocean thru the new planted trees — big beach with oasis & brick houses on sand Island a Saddhu flag on bamboo shack far down in the wind — up the beach half small — I went over later & found Kali or Vishnu? black image there — alone — back to Peter's injured 2'nd toe. Cut on a board nail — in Puri — pus — no medicines — all week the sand in the rubber shoe sandal — barefoot back to the Black Pagoda at sunset — & slept on wood table in hotel restaurant front on our travel bag pillow — now P has air pillow from Gary sleeping with long hair.

Shiv with little hard on over the Church door and all the little cocks shoved out by Man on girl over every window — Vishwamitra who screwed the pretty girl with his Santaclaus beard and brahmin string & big prick & white balls — squashed a bug — Will I pay that in Karma, — interruption — where am I? — was I — Caw Caw Kaw Kaw of crows along the beach road in Konerak — real Ravens — I gave one a peanut he didn't take the ants assembled on window ledge — he'd been picking at the garbage-bag in the barred window.

Out 9:30 AM after late ganja sleep — all day previous morn, then again night in room before sleep 3 sticks — this morn out to visit old temples — First Parisuramahesvera still looking like moving fuzzy tractor wheels — to Muktesvara "gem" walking around on the walls looking — then Vitale? it's like Venice names of chapels — These in provincial fields like French or Belgium chapels in the fields — Nataraj dancing with a hard on too — So the lover of Konerak is Nataraj, the six armed dancing Shiva — Ravanna shaking Mt. Kailash looking like a big germ or womb-spider because body broken away only spider-arms inside womb of rushing girls in Chaitya window stones — then out to fields Brahmeshvara & others Megeshvara with pools way out — always girls & some lovers naked with the man's member in the girls face or ass or pussy, very clean — broken arms some of them fading like ice statues, red sandstone — some intact with nipples & white or red balls — for breasts too — then back by the Tank Bindu and old temples in rear of town — grass & grey-black stone, towered with stone lotuses — Beautiful leaf-eared pink Ganeshes with broken trunks & supplicating mouse at foot of throne & fat round belly of Ganesh protruding out of his niche — bowlfull of sweets & prayer beads & other arms with noose & hatchet broken, the world snake twined round his shoulders & belly — one twined on his knee too — snake leg-bracelets — fat knees of elephant boy — baby — stone baby Ganesh — Wouldn't you think you'd seen the reverse of your hatchet this axerday — Miss Gannippatti, Parvati's his mother. That's enough. Riding busses in sunlight past three small ruined towers near the road — Past red stone wall & gate of Ramakrishna Math — "He eats meat & smokes in private" said Steven Koner about the Swami at the de luxe boarding Guest House. Lost on the vast lawns of Bubaneshwar, new capital — vast low buildings miniature from blocks of fields away — lights on thru the columns & glass window bricks — the huge wall & field, from which a bicyclist emerged onto the

Sunday nite road to the market — ate Fish Chicken Rice Cake Coffee soup butter bread 5 Rs. each — with Italian engineer in silk kerchief — charmed I'm sure.

*Eve 26th Nov. Bubaneshwar*

Washed clothes and bathed sunny early morning in the Bindu-sovar on the pitted red steps under the temple wall. A little Buck Rodgers temple with a lingam in the dim in-chamber below — washed red shirt & pajamas and undershirt & shorts & handkerchief & bathed my hair & swam, drying the clothes on a brick pilaster on the ghat jetty — then along the mossy stone back home in soft rubber sandals — out by Rickshaw to museum — one old statue of veined skeletal God with fiery topknot necklaced with skulls & a hideous fibre-grin from his skullface with rocks smeared off round his nose & mouth — a tinier image of same on the pedestal of the twined roof carving — seated — two armed with a mace? — (Like the lady with worms coming out of her split belly in the Louvre — down in the basement stairs — to the Slaves — are they still standing there against the wall in a big room arched passage littered with statuary? — ) Fucking started BC and continued inevitably to Konerak & after do continue but "died with the art of sculpture" said the young scholar in the palm leaf mss room in the Orissa huge-winged state museum modern air building — came from there to bus to Udayagiri caves & all day there rolling Kif & wandering reading guidebook or sitting looking out at filmy distances hills, the small temple Lingaraj in tree clusters in the distance — very much Far away and in French chapel landscape — Chapels in the fields anyway — the caves had some elephants bearing lotuses & mango branches in trunks — high naked black Jain Tirthankar 1960 statue upstairs on hill lovely young face — in one cave a sun flower I drew in little book but looked like

Rickshaw home & bus to Railroad at 7:30 — after reading Kabir aloud in cell for an hour — for ticket day after tomorrow nite sleeper 3rd class for Calcutta (reserved by telegraph from Bubaneshwar where we are) (Telly to Puri) (free) — on line at ticket window — waiting for nights Puri Express to depart — hip hip hooray a shout from throats at end of platform "Jai Jaiwan" or "Jai Jai Hind" or "goodby" in Orya — shouted over & over as the Squadron left by train for the Front — N.E.F.A. mountain chinese warzones — border troubles, sunflowers — thousands dead — 1500 — Home after supper & read papers & wrote & smoked.

*Next Day (Nov 27, 1962)*

Up 8:30 AM brushed teeth with minty cocainesque green toothpaste. Bus to Cuttack 9:30 AM & arrived in long U shaped miles long street, walking slowly up from bus stand end — passing silver filigree shops, cloth merchants with cheap paisley designed print bedspreads — blankets — Ate liver curry & eggs & fried fish & toast — stopped in to see dome shaped Muslim temple — tomb or Club What? — on way out a bearded turbaned long dusty-locked huge man with several cat's-eye rings — seated on a stone platform in the gate to the holy park — with his bearded friends — called me "Hey Babu, Babu" — we went back to them — one crushing ganja in his palm with his thumb — one dressed in bright green shirt and multicolored rag vest & green turban & long thin El Greco face — the third grey clothed & grey bearded — so we joined them — the big ringed man with round strong face motioned me to his mat — "Ganja!" I said and sat down, pulled out my early rolled cigarette & smoked — then they passed their pipe a long inverted miniature smokestack — with a pellet of rock inside to close the hole except to air — dragon fire leaping out of the top of the funnel clay, as they puffed & thick beards of white smoke emerged from their noses & mouth, dragging four, five times, and taking a long pull & letting out smoke and then taking deep draft, breathing in under his green turban with the light in the bowl reddening bluer — ah such a thin face & open eyes "I am a beggar" — as he took his leave briskly, Namaste & Salaam — we sat further smoking — talking little, "I read Kabir in English" — "Ah Kabir, great guru" They spoke a little English. Name, Moulana Baba — Mohamed Fakir? — "There are many much Babus in Bombay" — "Who your guru —?" — "I have guru — in X town." One (says Peter) was green vested with manycolored pockets & a green purse hanging that looked like a Vaishnav bead teller disguise — with which he left with green turban'd fellow. But the 4 or five rings on his friend's finger! And his own green ring, and one in black with a gold band around it, & one maybe in white. Then I waved my arm in a slow circle & fluttered my fingers like feet walking the long winding road to go. — They chased away the children watching, but first invited a little girl to smoke, then invited boys, & then said as all refused "All right go away & let us smoke our ganja in peace & stop watching & staring" — I saw a cop turban approach & retreat — Hafiz Rumi said Peter? & told of his travels in Egypt — Salaam — We had just before walked unseeing thru their gate home: "Permission for only three to live here in the gate" — others are transients, who are here. Been here 2 years — the heavy — Orson Welles eyes — said he was from Mysore, the south. He had black young santa claus face — Orson Claus — First fakir group I sat with, except the one in (North Bengal) Tarapith who was so lone, thin & asked for a rupee — reminded me of Bob Donlon — Smoked also ganja pipe like old habituée —

Where are all the old habituées of opium dens
in Calcutta alleyways

Where the short haired madwoman sits
chained to the curtained bunk in the
black brick wall —
Hear all the ringing of cymbals & drums &
the cries Hare Krishna
at worship down the night street in
Cuttack, candlelight —
Hurrying past to the bus — with a bearded demonic face
Philosophy Professor & his sister & bicycle — shouted "Beatnick," as we rode past — in Rickshaw from RR station chicken
curry meal — (after the police had called me in to ask for iden-
tification the second time —) rushed ahead to head us off at RR
to get our names — With Philosophy Prof. to his house a huge
garden, his short mother in Sari making us tea & sweets, brown
coconut soft balls candy — on the grass, translating his soft
poesy — "Naked in mirrors" — his painter friend's house & his
big drawing books of mustached cubist self portrait squares &
eyes — called in by police 3rd time, Prof. explained in Orya —
"nonconformist dress" — "with money" — This after the green
crazy Fakirs? I kept my peace this time having shouted angry
once "Wadya think, we look like Chinamen?" — "All these
recent Himalayan crises," you'll excuse the Police they said —
Maybe India already changing, war in the street in Cuttack —
back for tea in teashops & bus 6:30 back to Bubanishwar, home
& smoking & eating bananas & Peter tending a blister on his
foot with perfumed coconut oil.

*Cuttack*

At an hour late must be 9PM laying in second bunk of III'd class
sleeper reserved Bubaneshwar Calcutta (Puri express) high
again, on train, now swaying slowly & can't tell — yes just
moving in the stationary light — No not even moving, men
were moving on the platform thru dim window — Train was
still — dim whistle far away — humming, sighing into his bunk
— handing a butt stub to Peter to put out down in the bottom
bunk midst the giant bedrolls coiled like serpent scorpion with

107

black elephantiasis, wrapped in leather — back to morning woke & coughed up phlegm — bus to village Mr. Friman — of Chicago near Mandir (Ram Ram) — near Kapileshvara temple — 2 mi. south of Boob & divided by quarters into Brahmin Pandas, potters, sweepers, farmers bathing in the pool — we squatted by a small church chapel wherein the burlap blanket dark the leper Saddhu of that same village, who had been to Kedernath & Badrinath — emerged with his lip a dull blister & puffed face — hands & feet sore — cracked heel — pink fissure dirty — with whom we shared his pipe — I touched his feet to leave — who was shy & almost girlish "Been to a doctor no better" — "Says be cheerful says his guru develop a cheerful outlook — in every adversity" — Certainly cheerful later we saw him adorned in red cloth creeping walking to his additional image mandir, a block painted white — to give clean or fresh flowers & water on the Lingam or didn't see the image therein. Then bus & walk to Rickshaw to UTKAL university — modern architected to meet a philosophy lecturer who'd stopped us yesterday in Cuttack streets after we met the Fakir Babu by the gate. — All this writ with the train rackety & my feet crosslegged in a sheet, in bright light & the shifting of valise under seats — old man in bottom dark bunk says Ram Ram in quavery voice — thought before "the world is many things at once & not just one thing at a time after another." — P. just passed me up his cigarette — I laying in the bunk hardly energy or belief enough to rise & write it down except the keeping conscience of dreams and days as long dreams to be connected to be written in flashes — between breaths — puffs — shuffling of feet, reading aloud the war news, the radio in the tea stall at the wall of Lingaraja compound near the bus stand, night yellow electric weak bulb, I counted 30 loiterers listening to speeches or newscasts in Orya about NEFA & China-Ladack — the trains all over India speed on dark rails at once with lights on in the carriages, swaying from station to station, eclipsing the night & space 200 miles in yr sleep —

  I had fall'n asleep — thinking that Peter took cigarettes — so he going to head to smoke roll more — but he was in his bed — I was interrupted — I got up to pee & write & smoke & was writing and — bam banging on the locked sleeper door "There are vacancies" — I tried open the door — locked — ah yes, this very existence is nightmare — standing at the other end of the car like Bartleby leaning into the lightbulb.

Sat down in a single ample wood seat near the door & lavatory lights, at an open barred window — the dragon patterns of the scorpion stars — dark — and blur lights below the eyes, car lights moving across the sand, the creak of the car wheels slow & regular and thump every 4th second — to a halt. Metalscrape of brakes. Puri express running over an hour late — halted where? Stars outside.

Staring out the window — Einstinean wonders — the sensation of moving trains — the senses altering the blue night to a magic bowlful of fairy eternal stars — optic blue & yellow lights — like cigarette matches flaring — Whose bodies are we in? Bull or Scorpion what's the astrologic figures in dim gas pinpointed at joints or nerve spots in body bigger than cosmic buildings against the empty blue stage of endless air — space — back in bunk to think & sit. Peter now making another tea by the window seat.

Darker — Later — window — trees whirling past — rare lights by gates over water — red stations speeded by — watch houses — sparks — cough Stars — dim treelands steeped in soft cool darkness — Stars over Trees — I'll go way. Pee & sleep darkness — till next Scribulletin minute of Muckteshwar Sqwintillions of times. Who am I who am I the voice in my ear with the roar of the train. Looking in the mirror — Which eye will triumph, right or left? In the corridor by (Lavatory light — pen ran out)

*Calcutta* —

Landed in grey metal haze over Howrah bridge, walked over, the tide receeded & in the Sun mist silver mud, corpses wriggling — Walked aimlessly all day with big bag of mail & photo in Time mag and ganja smoking & eating Chinese, Salvation Army, YWCA breakfast — looking for hotel — wound up in dormitory

Salvation Army reading Newsweek Burroughs Review "insane genius?" — surrounded by Welsh and English coughers & Jokers — complaining & old jokes — "I saw all the Pathé houses in 1910" "Well I think today's my day to bathe" — 40 Rupees — "Go see South Pacific" — writing in bed — people wrapping up to sleep, phlegm in their voices, my eyes blurred neon.

One white haired gent talking about the "Saccharine content of beets — you've seen it in the Statesman, isn't it so — the white beet I think contains more sugar than the red." "This country's seen a lot of changes and she'll see more." "Terrible Corruption" — Sounds like half-echoed conversation from leather clubrooms or coal-collier foc'sle — "That is the process of evolution" — footsteps off, quavering voices — nearby Salvation Army Lights out 10 PM — was out on cement fire escape looking thru yards & whorehouses to street, blue nite.

*Calcutta December 3, '62 —*

Bought ticket to Benares for next Monday, so now near to leave.

In Chowringee hotel, 2 Chowringee corner Dharmatala St. — walking at nite home after visit underground drink shop Tari Coconut Wine white square bottles taste like yr own saliva, cool — Rolling ganja on the bark table there, a ladied Eunich in red Sari Dancing bells on ankles and cloth bust, hairy dance, arm weaving sideways down the head — and the one boy in velvet black jacket & in white clean pants shirt, whirling & snakey necked — slow arm gestures, palm up to the ear & over the Tibetan scalp mount — turning his head to and away from the twisting kid between his knees — facing him shaking his ass ruddy bottom I suppose in clean white pyjamas — Then to the urinal near the brick red government building by the huge no moon night tank enclosed with fence & hedges & the trams crashing by — around the back and in the dark high cubicle, men standing — one boy leaning against brick wall his young ragged face to the moon, in grey — an old fellow with scarf round neck — lots boys underground in Calcutta with scarfs wrapped over the head, face peering thru shawl-like — one tough — and the boy crost the way whose eyes met mine often, young as he drank with his friends, occult Indian hand-snake gestures patting his hair — he danced holding his hair side right down with palm — ah the dances of Tangiers & the Jewelry boys & the camp dancers at the horse hashish fair way out in the village ten miles from Pasteur Blvd. — Irving strolls there now eats at the Paris —

The Salvation Army cots hurt my back & kidneys — now sleeping harder mattress wood shelf bed — Esplanade street-lights out my first floor window above street — long rides thru the inkey black mist fuzzing the lamps at the end of the wide road blocks away — darking the tops roof sky —

Kneeling at Peters feet in red shirt my breast against his shirted breast nuzzling his warm skin, while he jerked me off — later sucked the great hot nipple of his cunt — in bed late morning 9 crowds rushing thru Chowringee to work — the cab speeding down the Blvd to the modern red airconditioned apartment where we left our knapsacks books tankas & Sarod & typewriter —

Asok, Sunil, Hope at table, tea — Then to Nimtallah — the half moon hanging cupped over the Howrah skyline — the tidal roar of Trams over the bridge a mile away down, its lights spanning the black Ganges to the rows of undecipherable litter-lights & the red yellow orange flag of Will's Gold Flake candled in the water — standing the other month there on the park jetty with high concrete balustrade, the wall roar of the tidal step of water rushing up toward us, staring over from the shore — I running lost my rubber sandals — in the ashy mud.

Smoke tonight really rolling white over the wall — a few Tues. Nite Circles of ganja smokers with flower heaps cupped in palmleaf cone wrap — familiar whiney saddhus putting red black 3'rd eye on my skull front — homage to Kali Ma — 30c NP. — 90 NP for 3 finger of ganja — No yellow 10 pack cigarettes — sitting in the square small noisy mandir at midnight — rolling ganja on the marble warm floor — charcoal stove of grey mud clay on bricks or stones — bright red coals & a pot of thin potatoes frying in ghee — I presented a box of milk boiled

111

sweets — Rasgoulas etc — white & wet in — the floor cardboard treasury — & O the beautiful chested snub faced large
matted hair muscular saddhu who I slept near, nights ago —
who when I passed last week & did not enter, motioned at me &
gave a fistful more prasad — white sugarcandy balls — as he'd
earlier given 3 handfulls when I slept near him, watching him
stretch on burlap with cloak round his radiant body — while
the Pandas splashed water in the court, so I was drove away —
into the burning ghat warmth, & stretched out on a marble bench
in the saddhus sleeping flop room or mourning alcove of white
marble, with the names of the dead written in bengali on the
brown creamy walls — Sunnil pointed at his own name writ
there a week ago — with the date of his father's death — so now
with Hope I — we all 3 sat down at the wall with saddhu crowd
& rolled & smoked & all ate prasad, I asked saddhu his guru's
name address and asked could I photo him later same day this
week to give photo to his guru in Benares he would be delighted
— all this thru Hope's Urdu translation — he gave me a great
garland of flowers — then after visit to red brick pavillion with
Bihar gang Chant drum cymbal Kirtan of midnight river light
freedom — ecstatic cymbal chorus rising & dropping down to
build again abruptly — voices shouting — and cries of youths
Hari Hari Bol (say Hari — Vishnu) (Say Name Hari!) — Name
the Name! — as they enter the Burning Ghat gate — several
corpses, one wrapped in white covered with flowers face hid
woman on rope charpoy — another man with bald, red painted
head & foot soles — waiting all alone nobody near, waiting for
the wood or hour to come move him into the bright red fire —
orange perfume — also riding in cab away, a procession, first
a few dancers & drummers & a fellow skipping backward showering small blossoms on the corpse path moving borne by group
of friend bearers, and some few mourners behind, the whole
Breughel Disney scene passing in an eyeglance from the fast taxi
window, they going we returning from the woodpile burning
court.

The lady in Puri on the sands, carried round & round the wood
pyre, a meager one so they lay her face down sleeping on her

arm extended out of the broken wood bed pile — and the fire
begins crackling under her chest & head — hair burning — by
the big oceanside near the local beach — a few dhoti'd saddhus
plain looking workers sitting in wall-shade talking & smoking
— red pipes — we lit ganja-cigarettes & smoked.

\* \* \*

The mushrooms are neither god nor not god.

\* \* \*

Hope typing letters to Home Ministry requesting review her
expulsion order.

NEFA-LADACK China India border war ended today said
Sunil Ganguli at Coffee House, — Sat. evening — I was sick
with genitourinary tract disasters — mild pain to pee & constant
peeing — calcium oxalate crystals aplenty, acidic urine so they
don't dissolve, consequently the sharp minute crystals irritate
the bladder passages cause pee unease & pain — a few many red
blood cells —

Down to the Coffee house meet Sunil & Shakti & others and
Sankar drunk and Derek Boshier — bored talking, walked down
Mahatma Gandhi road past grey sheeted sleepers in the arcades,
children sprawled brown naked buttocks on hag's arms, fires in
the gutter & crouched beggar refugees cooking pots above, a
woman rolling spices into red paste on the sidewalk, the bare
sidewalk itself her rolling board, grinding stone on stone in the
wet red patch by the curb — Under the bridge (carrying the
huge rolled calendar posters of Kali and Hanuman & Ganesh
& Shiva & Vishnu we bought six blocks away as they hung from
a lamp post) — Sitting listening to the bridge roar passing ganja
smokes around watching the leap-arch of the bridge narrow
across the water like flying roof to the Howrah Shore, calli-
graphed with red & white lights along the horizontal center —
discussing the space with Derek

Suddenly two black-coated red-crowned cops appear & take us
to the police station.

HOWRAH BRIDGE

Grey stones, dusk, arriving in rickshaw at Nimtallah, a great crowd & under the red brick shelter of the ghat pavillion, several different clashing bands of cymbalists & smokers ringing the walls with death-house chants —

All along the ghat side hundreds crowding — down the steps listening to song recital of prayers — the grey Gates to the burning ground thronged with mourners.

Dusk & the lights across at Howrah and violet illumination below them where the sun set.

Nearly a full moon hanging over Calcutta.

I passed along the row of burning corpses — a woman, thin & waving her arms like an insect, sat on ash pile near the few glowing coals — motioned me over to share her woe — later passed by & offered her change — she looked at the coins, accepted them & flung them away, forward into the next firepit where a bearded Saddhu crouched toasting his pancakes (little flat poories) in the fire ashes speckled with live coals.

Sat down with her then & held my tongue out (holding it with thumb & forefinger) to show I couldn't talk. She was stretched out across the white narrow pit, one side her thin behind, her thighs covered with a rag laid across them, the feet & heels sunk into a pillow on the other side — waving her arms over her head — Earlier a red-clothed saddhu with huge Shiva Trident like a pitchfork (so he looked like a devil all in red) had gone up & slapped her on the back. . . .

When I sat down she began talking Bengali — her right arm near the shoulder was cracked open, skin-broken & mottled raw wound with ashes in it — thin arm & opened her mouth her two teeth revealed gum tongue behind — she swept some coals aside from the lip of the pit where I sat & motioned me down. I squatted awhile & kissed her hand, then rose & went off.

On front of the adjoining mandir altar, a saddhu with high top-knot braid with red ribbon sat on blanket next to a big cow whose forehead had been touched with red for a 3rd eye — I saw many pass & put their finger on the cow's nose & touch their own heart or forehead as if in head-on salutation of politeness to the cow. The saddhu sat rocking back & forth, clanging an iron ring against the steel spoke he was holding on his lap, chanting & ringing steel on steel in time to the music.

One one burning pile, two feet were turned over by bamboo poles — feet detached from a body around the thighs — blackened, & the red fire burning around them.

Huge circle in the adjoining ash garden-singing with drum & small hand cymbals.

Tomorrow I go to Benares & this the last dusk-Sunday there, more crowded than I'd known.

*10 Dec 1962 10 or 12 PM*
*The Doon Express 3rd Class to Benares*

In the bathroom mirror staring at
    my black eyed face
peering thru dark gleaming hair
    my front thinning — all
of us to die
        letter scrawled with angel babe
        round halo-shine marks
   (Bill's short news — sending letters
day be leaving Calcutta —)
    in the train mirror
roaring om om on the tracks, the faint
    other universe howl inhalation
    ear esophagus grill —
       thought it was the which
        which of the Engine —
Hope running from place to place,
    consulate USIS
"I know her to be a maid or great lady
        — fine brow, noble mind — "
Smoking plain chain cigarettes, coughing crosslegged in my
    bunk, all the lights on and one blue glare protector, the
    silent moving dusty fans, — but a clean car bright rock-

ing along the rails to
       Kashi oldest in the world
           continuously inhabited city —
To invite Chou En Lai & Mao Tze Tung — To India — Nehru
alone — secret Dorothy Norman Interview — what questions?
Conspiracy in the magazines — Aether left behind — join the
common market — Conspiracy among nations, keep England
out — a political union — France independent — fine — Nobody presume — to star a war.

The world's development seems to make sense: a challenge to
live or die, unite and Not Perish, compromise, reject paranoia
about each other's motives' or thrash that out in Person on T.V.
— To a world television debate on Telestar — the race for
space —
       and death looming on every
soul in the planet
       that reads
       What America needs, "an alliance with China" —
       Democratic communism
— freedom of all people — to be guaranteed
   capitalist republics —
   Stumbling out of the bathroom I thought — Who got the
money & the big houses — as Jibananda Das asked before he
got run down by a Tram — Sad he not here —
           "Three beggars
     washing their hands in the grey wind,
     drinking the grey wind from their cupped palms
        on the corner of Bentick Street
     Downtown Calcutta near the
        Post office quiet wide street
     Three beggars over a pot
        cooking in the gutter charcoal —
     An old woman comes near, wanting
        the warmth of the Fire —
     And they gossip about who got the
        Houses of Calcutta,
     who won and lost all the money —

Crippled beggar and aide on Choudui Chowh, Calcutta

Foot severed
from body
along railroad
tracks

Hand and arm
beside tracks

Allen Ginsberg seated on ground beside beggar-man

Allen Ginsberg at Puri-Konarah temple ruins, 1962

Leper beggars lifting chilam (Ganja pipes) to lips on Dasawamedh
Ghat steps by Ganges, Benares, December 1962

A woman rolling spices into red spice on the sidewalk (see p. 113)

Sitting under Howrah bridge on the little promontory (see p. 59)

Peter Orlovsky with
guitar case pausing on
Howrah Bridge

Chaucer pilgrimage
folk on Howrah . . .
one near-naked
Saddhu stretched out
with his cane stick at
his side (see p. 121)

Allen Ginsberg on Calcutta street corner, October 20, 1962

Peter Orlovsky and Allen Ginsberg in Calcutta

Allen Ginsberg in Calcutta street

                    Who remembered thighs on the
                    bed of down — "

Accused with sleeping with everyone — a fantasy of marrying
Hope to keep her from harm — from the State — To keep her
free — What Shelley would do.

Over the boat into Ireland, over the rocking Train to Kashi,
Who got the power in China — Mao Tze Tung alone, Chou En
Lai — Mao must answer personally, is he Yevtuchenko's Stalin
on the telephone a Stalinist? The Stalinist line? Mao ought
write a poem on the border.

To meet on the border: Freeport Himalaya cities — Suggest
the U.N. ought to be built in the Himalayas — Dalai Lama —
Tibetan atrocity stories, true or false?

Print the documents — Hope's integrity lost, like 1810 Classical romances — the picaresque of the Pure Girl — I shoulda
gone to the police — write complaining — see Nehru — is he
isolated? —

                    Not that Shaggy! Sd Jerry Newman mad dog hairy
butter story — closing the door on the mistaken thought process
ambiguously knowing the exact shagginess of the word shaggy
posted to the London Times. This guy came from New York with
a god in an airplane — to take Mescaline poetry in Greece —*

Is Mao Capt. Claggart? Nehru be Billy Bud? Doomed like any
skeleton in black flesh cooking rice by a bustee in Calcutta Chinatown, leaning against fence — The industry factory in the
open space inside — outside street full of cabs & push huge
barrows of 2 wheels & bamboo flat floor over the wet cobbles
past the concrete roofless garbage bin on the corner — picking
among the grey garbage — weaving hooped white baskets —

Baby crying on the train and letters in my lap & notebook on
Jack's explosion.

---

* One day Terry Newman bought *London Times* at the NY Public Library &
read Lost & Found ads, "Reward for big white shaggy dog," and found big
white shaggy dog on 5th Avenue, so he bought London plane tickets for him
& dog & arrived at house in Grovsnor Square, butler opened & peeped out
at them coldly saying "But not that shaggy" & closed the door.

                              119

Everybody afraid to intervene — the people intervene —
Positive Program for Peaceful Progress
1. Red China representative in slacks take seat at UN next summer
2. Dalai lama send a representative, in robes.
3. International legalization of kif, ganja, marijuana, cannibis, hashish, Bhang.
4. Telestar TV Debate with Kruschev, Kennedy, Mao & Nehru at UN together translated into all languages — on the Radio & all papers, before stadium audience or in a New UN glass heated city in Himalayas, with all year roads — way station on the way, railroads, road. Hitch hiking stops & big hostel —
5. Invention of a miniature transistor sending-receiving T.V. station attuned to near-infinite numbers of possible stations, one set to each person in the world: Central Sender's only one among many. A vast industrial project with world sharing of food: UN Committee to technologize world agriculture 50 billion a year apiece US & Russia —

If necessary U.S. get one car every 4 years. Only apiece. Perfected machinery so sweet humming auto (hand tooled) lasts for good — for 30 years — like any human thing, we can build all the rockets, why not better & more cars — small cars & motorcycles — rebuild the city streets to handle — cut down the population by diaphragms & rubbers insisted & given free to all by the U.N. The only identity, a diaphragm card — & how to end passports.

One law for all the World — Delegation of Sovereign rights. Free universal election of the world president — Nominated by countries?? How machine the elect world president
Everybody conspiring
Damn do you mean to say the world won't HAVE to have a friend?

The train stopped at Burdwan?? I'm confused. Train whistle & the man beside me groans & dead Céline in pocket Journey still telling the truth as he thought —

120

Then finish and to see what burning ghats at Kashi? and what
naked men at the river — and what charred legs and pelvis
turned over by bamboo poles into the center of the fire?
That Howrah om roar always the
 Sound of Doom to Come
sd/Derek and the echo in my
 own mind of the diminishing
 steel roar as Tram
 wheels clashed on tracks of
 humming concrete & steel —
Those pictures of the Chaucer pilgrimage folk on Howrah —
Sellers of combs, fortune tellers, monkey men, cardplayers,
astrologers, shoeshine, one near-naked saddhu stretched out
with his cane stick at his side on the broad walk across — a
team of huge black buffaloes pushing across the asphalt hill to the
center — where we rode tonite in a horse cab piled with knapsack & Sarod & the two girls — thru the black mist of early
night to the Huge Howrah Station and the crowds on the platform & the rush with baggage to find the right reserved bunk
shelfs & push the coffin-Sarod case under the seat & the striped
umbrella & typewriter, Peter's Knapsack in the aisle — sitting
in bunk writing & reading Céline, my head bent under the roof
of the rocking car.

. . .

*Benares: First nite out walking —*
 Stumbling between fire & cow at burning grounds.
 Staring at cow's udder the cow jumped up all 4 legs at once
nervously.
 Cows (11) wandering in Manikarnika ghat at midnite under
full moon, eating the rush ropes of the corpse-litters left behind
on the sand near the woodpiles on which corpses wrapped in
white cloth are burning.
 Took the wrong bus home, feeling proud I'd so quickly mas-
tered the bus system — only come to Kashi Station not Canton-
ment where we were staying.
 Dressed in western clothes black sweater & lumberjack shirt
in the chill night.

121

Walk along ghats, past umbrellas & sleepers up & down steps to the burning ghat.

High bright ringing of bicycle rickshaw bells on empty streets at midnight, the rickshaws racing down the inclined street curving past stores answering each other's bell rings.

The dark Rembrantian buffalo head & shoulders blinking staring out of an alcove — a live buffalo in a dark niche.

Hanging around the burning ghats, level on level of sand shelf, near a staircase saw a red round pot used for damping the fire when body's burnt away — I saw the pot near the wall on the first stair, & said to myself "Wow the old pot" thinking of the pot that the psychoanalyst stept on in Nimtallah — and avoided this — thinking "Sooner or later I'll step on break pot too." — & squatted down to overlook a burning corpse — staring down from the wall. 2 minutes later some one else — Indian mourner in scarf in cool nite air — smashed the pot with his foot. Later I heard the sound of clay crashing again when I threw away the cup used for milk I'd drunk.

And heard the same high sweet chime of Midnight that reminded me (listening in the ghat to the Benares tower) of Lima Peru R.R. Sta. clock "Struck before & never again — both."

*Benares — Vernasi Dec 12, 1962*

In Tourist office, white room with posters, Kanchenjunga, Tibetan Lamas blowing long curved horns with vast white mountain ranges beyond leading up to clouds of snow at glacier's foot — Walked out on Ghats along Ganga broad waters; — now perfect blue moon — night — like Venice, stepping on stairways up & down thru gates & over slabs of round concrete at water's edge, — going I saw a stairway down, I walked one level above it all along the waterfront — saw a ragged man stooping down the stairs head burnoosed in winter scarf — passed on to the burning ghats & there squatted and thought of the word Squat, what would next happen, — turning over a black doll-like small charcoaled corpse — of a child with thin legs, a dwarf — smoke in my face — acrid smell of musty wood, musty bone all the same — walked round, past the row of watchers squatted on a wall supervising the actual level where the fires were — the stairwell to the water side-wall — wandered up in Cupola overlooking the levels & fires & sat & smoked & brooded — walked over to see a cow reclining on 4 legs, head up eyes open, ear lifted when I said om softly — then back thinking of Venice along the De Chirico high Gnostic Walls — like Grenada — returning

I meant to review all that went on last nite — couldn't remember and listed events separately in the order of recollection — "Minarets & moonlit towers" — suddenly found myself all the way down along a path that almost disappeared at waters edge (like at the foot of rocky cliff wall walking home with Peter along the Indian Ocean side — at Mombassa from the small dhow piers port — Dhows from Arabia and Kutch and Oman — on the seasonal breezes) — so I was down at waters edge, saw a brick stairway leading up & as I mounted it to the top recognized I was back on the earlier level with long esplanade almost of pyramid staircases along the high embankment of Ganges covered with small temples and stone pandit's umbrellas — realized I'd walked back up the same staircase to the river I'd earlier seen (passing by & wondering the fate of it below). A man in burnoose scarf around his head descends slowly into the shadow — what'd he do there I thought Jack thought too — .

*Dec 13, '62*

Out with Peter Thurs. nite to Manikarnika ghat. Sat on stone ledges above the ash sand shelf filled with woodpile fires aburning, cows putting their big nose heads near under the foot of the pile bed — flame lighting his forehead, eye most closed, chewing some yellow stalks of straw kindling — boy chased three cows out of the rectangle garden of fire — they were eating up a corpse litter prematurely — or horsing around in the way — the nearby corpse masked in white shroud lay back in the flames & turned black, knees hanging down, the veil burning away and one ear sticking too far out, later became a thin black mummy

123

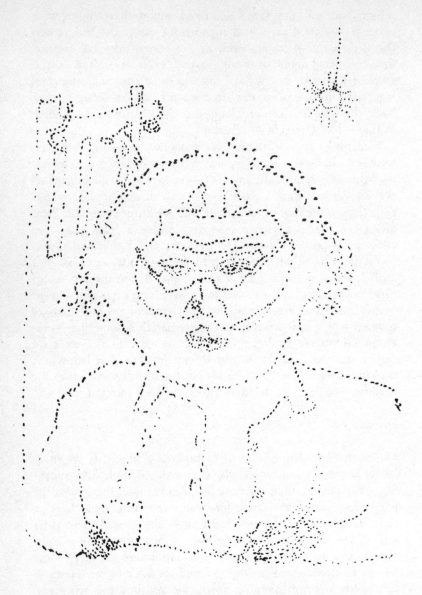

*Regional Tourist Office Rest Room Mirror, 13 Dec, 1962*

124

in flames — the furthest we saw lit up, later the bamboo attendants thwacked it in the middle and turned it face down in the
flames, skull hanging over the side in the fire — the middle
corpse had burnt thru the belly which fell out, intestines sprang
up (that is) like a jack in the box charcoal glumpf — then its
right leg and foot came up in silhouette as the pole boy shifted
it to the top first, then the other leg and foot spreading big toes
was poled up and over bouncing like a soft log — and his hand
(or hers it seemed to have a charred bracelet round the forearm)
slowly lifted from the chest as the bulk burned — fires playing
orange around from black cranium along the sides, over the lifted
hand — and the two feet flung back over detached and burning
over the middle of the bed — like burning fear away — I
thought, burning the dross inside me — Dogs curled asleep on
the shady steps as the moon rose over the western sky with
Orion near, and the flat plate of Ganges stretching up to the
faraway river shore beach — fires reflected in the waters as we
went away, white mist reddened flaring out over the water,
blocked by the huge castle embankment steps & high Dharmashala of brick where the dying came to spend last days breathing
smoke.

*14 Dec 1962*

Eating a banana yesterday — fine white creamy ripe cheap
banana — I said to Peter "Nature is certainly a good cook."
Actually I said "Nature is a good cook."

This afternoon sitting in high red stone balcony overlooking
Manikarnika burning ghat — watching as the body was poled
upright so it fell out of the fire by mistake & lay down all black
in the dirt — the pole boy's mistake — he poled it up with a
great shower of sparks & jumped away blinking to get aside
from the blast of heat — then his guru pole man came by, stuck
his pole thru the side of the carcass & adjusted it on top of the
fiery bed — the head pillowed on black firewood.

Found a room to live in, stone floor with huge doors everywhere opening the walls out on 3rd story to trees, monkeys,

125

market below one side, beggar street to ghats on the other side, many shelfs in the wall for images & books. 43 rupees a month.

*Saturday 15, Dec 1962 —*

Moved into black & white high 3'd floor room — 9 great doors, three on each side North South West and long balcony my own North and South with chicken wire grill protection from monkey peoples that clamber nearby roofs — bought straw mats, clay pots for storing water, a tin pail — installed bright 100 watt lightbulb & statue wood Chaitanya & Peter his red bellied Ganesh with 3 delicate eyes in alcoves above the doors — listening to transistor radio Peking — shot some morphine-atropine to relax, on a charpoy (rope bed on wooden frame) plenty blankets for cool winter in Benares — a desk and shelfs to hold accumulated mss. and notebooks — feel at home & happy.

*Sun Dec 16, 1962 —*

Long walk at dusk from the orange Raj Ghat bridge shimmering in sunset water, along the ghats waterfront — huge walls & towers & rocks & balconies — a prospect along the bend of the river like Venice along Grand Canal or seen from Judecca — finally to Manikarnika burning ghat stopped awhile looking down on Sunday crowds — tho sparser than Calcutta's Nimtallah — and in along Vishiwanath Temple lane to the main roads. Visited a powdered milk factory. Roar of rr trains over the Raj Ghat bridge a mile or more up the river — sound reflected down the waters at night like airplanes or tidal-bore nature groan. Tin pan drumsound coming from street below our balcony — puja (worship) at some small shrine around the corner in an alley at 9 PM. Blake life-mask photo on a nail on the wall between the balcony doors.

*Dream — 12 PM —*

In a hospital or store corridor in Benares — a young lady, a

nurse in white low breasted dress and long hair, with cap, I see
she has white powder on her breast and is a helpful saintly lady
— I say "That white Powder — you look like a saddhu in a
burning ghat — ash smeared like that, what for? how charm-
ing!" and she looks at me, annoyed and says, "what do you
mean, ash smeared? That's talcum powder in case you're so
naive you don't recognise it" — and she begins kissing me very
kindly on my ear, & then full lipped on my mouth, which feels
very soft & sweet & gentle, and I say "well I'm sorry I didn't
mean to insult you" — and she says "you shouldn't say things
like that to us girls" and goes on kissing me so boldly I'm
ashamed of myself, thinking such dreamy stereotyped ascetic
thoughts about everybody — and goes on kissing me, I feel her
warmth & a funny kind of eternal intelligence & liveliness about
her — and I say "Well if you want me to shut up & not say what
I think ... but you did have so much powder there & that's
what it reminded me of" and she says "Why, you" and just
keeps on kissing me. She's a friend or nurse friend of Dr. T.
Leary I believe in the dream. And she kisses me like Peter on the
mouth so I'm delighted and amazed. And think well I must
bring her home to Peter she's such a nice girl by gad. And woke
up giggling and delighted. Waking I realize the approach was,
roughly, as L . . . . . movie — the girl the same as eternal
feminine of Amazon Yage sweetness recollection — Shiela,
Francesca, Marilyn, anyone — Remembering as a child on Haledon avenue I said to a girl (with her armful of books coming
home from School #12) my what a big bust you have — and
she hit me & chased me home, her face red with annoyance &
embarrassment — and that silly drama must have been the
Great Freudian Trauma that turned me against girls ever since
— sort of a silly denouement of decades of homosexuality — a
scene like that that really bugged me out & I was always
ashamed of — my naivete — to have such a lasting effect on me
— yet that's about all there is to it — this girl in dream acting
the opposite in such a nice way I woke thinking By god look
what I've been missing!
    A woman in the street below balcony on the Ghat — whom

I wanted to give money to earlier today — who was shrieking last night at 4 AM in the darkness, while another saddhu wraped in burlap nearby countered her outraged high voiced complaints to the empty street by moving his prayer beads under his burlap blanket & shouting for an hour "Ram! Ram! Hari Krishna Hari Ram!" I had got up on the balcony, shivering, to watch them last nite & earlier tonite — and even now while woken up writing her voice is loud arguing on the street still. Kali Ma.

Also the thin armed lady sitting in an ash pit in Nimtallah — the gentility of her gesture, throwing away the few coins worth 3c I offered her, thinking she was a crazy woman — as she motioned me to join her — with her wounded ash smeared cracked skin near the shoulder — an amazing saint there — nothing to ask or offer but the kindness of ashes & wails for understanding that —

Leary, L . . . . . , the sunyassini in the burning ghat, the lady beggar yowling on the street, Clark Gable & sleeping close with Peter warm under blankets, the memory of Pucallpa vision of rejected women, and the old traumas of Paterson — all recalled at once on waking up.

*17 Dec '62*

Long walk this morn to Manikarnika ghat — sat inside red stone porch with Saddhus & smoked ganja pipe & inquired about guru of good looking saddhu from Nimtallah — reminiscent red haired Naga saddhu knew him. Cow laid its head on my lap to be scratched. American tourists floating by in rowboats.

— — —

Dream: I meet Buddy Isenberg & Burroughs — turns out Isenberg is a nice girl — we sit at cafe table & talk, I apologize for writing so late. Nice dinky soft mannish looking girl. My demeanor is excessively self assured, is demeanor. Strange I should dream twice of girls in one day. "At my age" I said to Peter.

This morning while my back was turned from the table I heard a great thump — turned around to see a monkey jump on

128

the table loaded with oranges & bananas, snatch one banana & leap out to the balcony, disappearing thru the lavatory window — next sitting on high branch of adjoining tree peeling the banana & staring at me thru the big leaves.

Incense in the room tonite, bought straw mats to cover half the slate-black tile floor.

\* \* \*

What Vanity? What possible divine
blessing on all this Politics.
What invocation beyond Millions
of Votes for 1960 Hopes
What rat Curse or Dove vow slipt from my hands
to help this multitude
Smirking at the ballot box, decieved,
sensible, rich, full of onions,
voting for W.C. Williams with one
Foot in the grave and an eye
in a daisy out the window

*18 Dec '62* —

Sitting on rock at Harischandra Ghat — down below a sand slope at the water's edge blackened with ashes, a high pile of firewood ablaze and a man's head bent back blackened nose & mouth unburnt, black fuzzy hair, the rest of the chest belly outlined along down thighs at top of the pyre, feet sticking out the other end — now turned toes down — cry of geese & rabble of white longnecked good goose swan boids pecking in the water's edge a few feet from fire.

Nearby scows filled with sand from the other side of the river, laborers carrying baskets of grey sand up the brick stairway from the river — "Oh — the head's going to fall off — " The pile darkening, white ash floating up — a few watchers squatted on bricks facing the pyre — Pole man comes & tucks a foot into fire — then circles around & pushes length of pole against the black head (lain back with open black throat & adam's apple silhouetted against the small flames against the green river) til

129

the body's balanced on the center of the collapsing charred logs. Donkeys led along the sand path, children running with kites, a black baby with no pants & pigtails, balancing a stick of bamboo — A saddhu in orange robes sitting up on a stone porch on the embankment under turrets of an old small castle — rather Venetian the scene — Rectangular-sailed boats going down stream — the air above the pyre curling in the heat, like a transparent water veil between my eyes & the greenfields & trees along the horizon on the other side of the Ganges — and the embankments, red temples spires, toy mosques, trees and squat white shrines walling in the bend of the river upstream to the long red train bridge at Raj Ghat an inch high.

\* \* \*

*18 Dec* and a torn burlap bag to cover the squat pantsdropd lavatory window that opens on the staircase of the house, so ascending passersby can see the diarrheic mud bubble down from the asshole of P. Orlovsky & Company, Inc.

This morning down to the burning ghats & sat with same group of sadhus in their eyrie in the sandy basement porch of a pilgrim's rest house — fire with a pot of boiling lentils, embers from the burning ghat down below at 10 AM — a trident and bamboo lance & brass water-pot begging stoup scattered around, one friendly Sadhu named "Shambhu Bharti Baba" with whom I've sat and smoked before — today seeing my difficulty handling the red clay pipe he made & accompanied me smoking a cigarette mixed with ganja — I also partook of two pipes tho I coughed & the cold snot bubbled out my nostril from the strain-wheeze — brought some bananas & green seed fruits to distribute, gifts — and camera so made photos — the Naga Sadhu (S b b) wanted his very confusingly, as he don't talk but makes finger gestures — he got to his feet, stripped off his g-string & pulled down his cock under between his legs — one yogic ball bumping out — like cunt — for a photo — I took a dozen, all the group smoking round the pot & ashes — one standing of the Naga sadhu with his pots & brass tridents etc. then high put on my shoes & walked back along the ghats home, & slept in dark closed room a half an hour — read Mayakovsky

130

elegy to Lenin — "and
            child-like,
                wept the grey-bearded old"
and Brooklyn Bridge poem — I didn't remember it was so lovely
— "in the grisly mirage of evening
. . . the naked soul
                of a building
    will show
                in a window's translucent light"
— — —
Jodrell Bank's deposit of heavenly radio waves
— — —

   Shot some M, last nite, up on mattress reading The Statesman
(Calcutta), Time, Mayakovsky, writing postcards, washing
socks handkerchiefs undershirt, Peters cock, necking with him,
   While below the balcony under the streetlight one milk shop
clattered pails
   in the darkness, the Desasumedh Ghat beggars kept thin fingers moving under dried burlap, counting beads Jai Ram Jai
Citaram, & the woman on the opposite corner with
   long wild hair crouched against a bidi shop steps rocking back
& forth — I gave her 25 NP when I went out before dawn to buy
milk & cigarettes —
   now the square begins working — I feel like An American in
Paris in 1920 — The naiveté of neighborhoods awakening,
radios turned on too loud to the Hindi news in the milk shop,
   First lights turned on across the street, in the Cigarette and
fried noodle peppers stall at the gate of the market,
   three rickshaws circling to take off up street and look for cold
dark business
   Householders wrapped in shawls carrying brass waterpots
trudging into the Ganges steps, passing & observing the beggar
man in the mid-street shrouded in his own burlap shawl — he'd
moved all night praying —
   and carrying flowers to adorn the Lingams in the temples
overlooking the starlit, planet-lit river —
   arguments between Ram & Cita in Hindi voices tinnily ricko-

131

chetting all the way up to my balcony from the radio —

Walkers coughing & trudging river street in Paterson too at this hour —

Him crouched under street lite on the corner counting a basketful of small potatos

Such a basket as I bought last night to contain my bananas & oranges, from white glued paperbags written in ledger sheets Hindi another day in a dark office —

Martial music to accompany the morning's broadcast, and the sound of a claxon with a throat inflammation in the background —

Peter lying dressed up in pants on mattress picking his red mustache, with long hollywood Christlike hair & Christ's small beard stubble —

I found out Octavio Paz is in Delhi the Ambassador of Mexico, arranging train rides for his tennis team — a headache —

Blake's photo on the wall, waiting waiting waiting — with his life mask eyes closed — thinking — or receiving radio messages from the cosmos source —

The rickshaw wallahs had slept all night crouched covered with their shawls on the red leather slope plastic of lowered rickshaws —

at night their bells rang in tune back & forth, speeding down the hill to Godolia from Chowk, up & down answering alarm clock tingalings in the dead streets — an iceman's tingaling, a knife sharpener's charged bellsound —

A huge black tree looming over my window obliterating half the square, all nite lights shining thru its leaves from milk shop where a vat of white cow buffalo lact bubbles over a charcoal trench.

Coughs answering back & forth across the square, and the splash of the streetcorner waterpipe faucet, clearing the throat near dawn —

a big white cow with horns had walked slowly up the street alone, looking for something to do — cows all last night in repulsive play, chasing each other in the traffic to lick the red asshole pads they drop streams of urine thru on the puddled

street — black bulls horning the girls in front of Sardau's Hindu
Hotel, separated by silver giant wire trees, knobby with ceramic
eyes —

Wet charcoal & first white smoke impregnating the air to the
tops of the trees — the monkeys asleep — the weasles aware —
few rare ants — cigarette ashes cleaned from the trays in paper
bag on the porch with banana & orange peels (the cows' lot)
waiting the sweeper

Morning not yet come, Dec 19, 1962 must be 4 or 5 AM in
Benares, writing & fingering my cock & remembering Shosta-
kovitche's dead March as the radio bounces & crashes across
India with brass violins —

The smell of frying meat cakes and potatos, Jai Citaram in a
toneless voice, & gentle gossip near the rickshaws, the clanging
of a temple bell at worship time early a few blocks away.

A lady already arrived with small baskets of parsley & radishes sits in the road where it turns down to the river steps,
coughs & spits on the ground & bides in the gloom as the first
blue light breaks open clouds in the East sky over the river, seen
from balcony thru trees and a few balconied chickenwired houses
leaning over the steps.

The present is sufficient subject like Cezanne "I turn my head
this way or that an inch, & the composition changes."

and a high voiced automatic chant from one man emerges up
from the street amidst the voices of first male gossip & the lighting of matches as the morning walkers glide back & forth &
accumulate — but not a hatchet, I didn't accumulate a hatchet,
only straw brooms & mats & baskets & no more.

*19 Dec 1962 —*

Well, where now me, what next,
lying here in the church gloom naked mattress
like a Corpse under Covers, just come into Peter's mouth
with his cock in my mouth and pubic hair spread on my beard
cupping his soft ass halves with my palms —
now alone with all the french doors closed & darkened

133

in late afternoon against the skull drum & girl cry of streets of
    Market below my balcony —
What next soul task, in all this morphined ease
drowsing to wake at midnight in the oldest city in the world —
no need to rush out and carry burlap bags full of dung to make
    money
my checks arrive from around the world,
enough to lay here Oblomov all my fourth decade on the planet
with the stars rising and falling and half moon
disappearing as I peep out the blinds some nights weeks hence
reappeared hanging over the wrinkled old river —
rush out by airplane Vancouver New York Moscow
and shout & weep before mind gangs of new kids born between
    wars
with the tan red stain on my index finger dying deeper, cigar-
    ettes & tea
in too many Cafes from Santiago to Kyoto —
What possible poem to imagine any more, who can't
even read Blake or Kabir with two hours rat minded light-
    hunger —
Now seem the thrills of scanning the scaly dragon dream universe
equal in endlessness boredom to passing my moons playing Cards
in third class trains circling the equator, thinking letters to write
or creating a network of poetry slaves drugged by the lunacy of
    electronic brain meat —
or simply going home & sitting in the backyard watching the
    cherry blossoms fatten on my tree —
having to pay no taxes to anyone, mumbling in my bedsheets
    while
the same car lights of childhood prison the decade on my ceil-
    ing —
perhaps even dream up a monster God in the spotted whorls of
    vast eyeball —
My cup runneth over, my speed spilled into one familiar soft
    mouth
month after month, as if another birth won't connect life
together after death, all be black beforgotten from before —

Not even doom, not even Hell except what this is already
my mouth dry and having to get up & go out in the chill twilight
    to take a pee
trying to write a poem — whatever that could be,
scribbling in a vast book of blank pages, hoping my death will
    make sense of chaos notations —
dashes which lead only to the next consciousness trying to shake
    itself and be free
like a vulture circling over a green donkey field, like Lenin wag-
    ging his beard
and raising his index finger into the air to signal the rag-booted
    masses
a new Futurity! Archaic Eden and electric Serpent and my soul
    Eve
Curious over the fruit before her face, noisily humming with
    radio messages inside.
Poetry's the old apple tastes of death's tasteless eternity,
Morphine worm that eats itself — Peter goes to fetch chicken
    Tanduri
from the rickshaw thoroughfare a mile away — he's got his
    body out on the streets
in alleys with bright bulbs and cloth patterns, and plaster Vish-
    nus lying on a painted snakey bed — the same endless-
    ness
that wandering leads me mornings to the stone porch and the
    trident and fire & pipe
and naked saddhus who don't talk, crosslegged smoking dope
    to overlook the corpse meat-dolls
people bodies bursting and black-charred falling apart on log
    woodpiles by Ganges green fields
morning down below long bridges in the distance filling empty
    space half thousand miles
to familiar Calcutta filled with newspapers and war and burning
    trams
by railroad stations where soldiers wave from trains at homeless
    lepers sleeping months on huge concrete floors.
India's hopeless existence, repeating the name of the Lord in the

Kali Yuga, begging workless disconnected from rocket
     dams bursting over the torrential mudpie oceans —
We'll be on the moon before I die, & maybe eat bread on Sat-
     urn —
receive some heavenly message radio waves at Jodrell Bank —
     escape in the mind
to rearrange the molecules of existence to a new Kaleidoscope
     China —
See perhaps beautiful yellow cheeks and brows, new bellies to
     dominate the four
directions of space & fill up time with their fried Pork Chow
     Mein —
even if everybody eats Peking Duck with orange sauce, and has
     two children
won't life be as useless as ever?  But I wouldn't know anymore
     — what others should do
with the vital breath, and the lungs and testacles we have all
     been given —
Once I thought to rebuild the world to supreme Reality
Emulsive consciousness developing in national brains and fac-
     tories incandescent with human toys —
What, robots with light bulbs to do our dying for us? — eat our
     steak, and let us fuck them too —
Once I thought the cracked walls of the mortal house peeled
     back, beneath the spectral plaster
saw the vast Bauhaus built in God by God for God in Man —
Once I thought that by laughter & patience, by not scheming,
     by no ascetic sneer,
the giant radiostation of eternity would tune us in to an endless
     program
that broadcast only ourselves forever — now I hear the ringing
     of gongs and skull drums in Hindu temples,
cries on the streets, peasant women waving sticks at hungry
     cows, the light bulb burning white
only so I can transcribe the wierd suffering details
for whom to read, myself & my fond dying indifferent trapped
     fellows —

Ah — in comes Peter with two big dead stuffed chickens to eat.

## I I

So we ate cold chicken squatting on a mattress, 25 rupees 5 dollars worth while the old lady beggar I been watching on the corner steps downstairs rocked back & forth on her heels for the 4th successive day. Sleepless as last night no sleep, & all morn feeding bananas to monkeys on the roof at sunrise & then to Police to give papers registration address — the policeman a jolly type baffled by our presence: "Why do you want to stay here in India so long?"

Baffled myself out on the balcony staring down at the evening crowds and lights, a gang of cows & bulls burping angrily — gathered together munching the dried refuse of leaf-plates piled near the corner water pump. I stared in wonder — are they all walking corpses? At the burning ground the bodies are just the same, only they're not moving, they're dead corpses, here — all these gongs being rung & cigaretts sold across the road — and along came mincing an Indian devotee with the step of Quepie Doll Hugh Herbert, & he was covered with flowers round his neck, carrying a brass tray of little white sugarballs (god food. Prasad) — approached by a beggar he stoped gaily & dug up a palmfull of candy, gave it to outstretched hand, & went mincing his way on the concrete path to the river, to temple probably to mind his evening before sleepdeath tonite. "They're all mad" I said to Peter, "Chinese invasions indeed!" They'll see some kinda Chinese invasion aint been seen any old thousand years ever.

## I I I

In bed all day recovering awake from sleepless nite 3/4 grain M — going on & off balcony to stare down at street — Bulls grunting, they eat offal & garbage — some sleep in the concrete garbage dump tanks on Godowlia Corner —

Processions of rat-a-tat drums marching down the street — straggling behind big drum, four coolies bearing posters advertising a hot romantic movie — fat hero with big tits & double chin & Indian movie queen with round cheeks — "Kum Kum"

137

— and a whisp of hair arranged over the eyebrow — a child ahead banging cymbals.

Or a marriage procession in yellow & orange silk the groom, his long shirt tied to bride's veiled sari figure followed by a dozen ratty relatives & a couple of wheezing old beggars banging on drums rhythmically.

or several times a day on the street a small group carrying a shoulder-high bamboo litter with a corpse swathed in orange or white shroud — saying aloud the gang Jai Citaram or Ram Nam Ram Nam — threading their way thru slow moving cows, rickshaws abycicle, hand carts with huge wheels, oxcarts dragged along by wood yoke to the ox-hump — the procession to the burning ghats passing down a main street or into little streets & thin alleyways crowded with potato chop stalls & teashops & portable salt-snacks, bearers carrying wicker baskets of brown dry hot noodles & roast peas.

Went down for milk & cigarettes — at the tobacco stall always greeted by Jai Guru or Jai Hind — I reply Jai Tarama or Jai Krishna or Jai Citaram & namaste clasped hands to brow or breast, clutching cigarettes & matches in one fist.

The dood (milk) shop, mixer salesman squatting barefoot on a wet stone board, pouring tea & milk from aluminum cup to glass or clay pot — the local dogs "fried in ghee" — mangy Breughel curs with gentle manners, three dogs living together in the milk stall alley each has an injured foot & pink flesh showing thru scarred, ribbed dogbitten flea buzzed hairskin. One dog walks on 3 legs, the left back leg retracted up above the level of his balls, as if a spasm came & left it tied up there — barks with hideous gargle at rival dogs invading his milk shop pavement territory — licks up the charcoal-milk-cow-piss-dishwater running in pools in the broken concrete. I gave him some milk several days ago.

I had chicken bones to dispose of in a Quality Restaurant box — sneaked him a handful and as I left heard the snarling & yipes of a 4 dog fight — I sneaked guiltily around the Ganges side street market looking for a trash barrow to leave my cannibal bones hid from Hindu Paranoiac gazers.

138

Sat & drank nice warm milk & watched the big white cow (always stealing vegetables in broad daylight from the gang of peasant women with baskets of herbs) lick the mangy three legged dog's neck with his big wise tongue.

*Dec 22, 8 PM —*

Walking (in dhoti & lumberjack shirt) thru Benares alleyways, turning corners past toy stands, thru red gates up Vishwanath alley past the temple — thru a grate seeing crowd round the lingam chanting slow-beat of drum vary-voiced tuneless mass — beautiful harmonies, ending as I passed out the back courtyard past the huge stone cow, with acceleration of drums — past the square where in daytime sell red and blue & yellow bright colored powders displayed in cones of dust —
down to Manikarnika ghat (with small photos of Howrah & Naga saddhu naked in pocket — to show him — arrived on street thru woodpile up alley down steps to take a crap by riverside, pushing aside open rear of my dhoti, sick diarrhea, washing my skin on the steps of river (with left hand?) No, right —
then up to Dharmashala sand-floored base level & sat in circles with Sadhus & a university bursar & the Naga I knew & silver haird fellow with boxer's or alcoholic's face but he cold sober smoking ganja by firelight — logs from burning pits brought up in clay dishes or iron tongs, still red & shining in square ash bed banked with sand — Shiva trident in ground — Sadhu came over; saw pix asked me to send him — to some difficult address in a Calcutta ghat — I promised — Sat smoking pipe (coughing firesmoke blown & my eyes watering & nose running) then moved over against wall on straw mat, touched Sadhu Naga's foot & conversed w/ English speaking Bursar —
then after long hour by fire, started home, blue sky specked with stars, there was Orion's belt near in the sky — I squatted to pee over a high stone path right down into the river, with bubbing noise falling down the 15 feet —
as squatting to pee
on the night Ganges —

139

Back there the firelit ghats.
Looking back I saw the several log fires burning orange, noticed
& remembered it to record, as Haiku.

By home — an argument between a Hindu w/ club & a blue
turbaned Sikh — crowd circled — up the street the prone body,
rag covered, can flat on ground a few feet away — one lit a
match to her head, new shaven a few weeks ago — blood trick-
ling down skull — a "motor" accident.

*Christmas, 1962*

## TAJ MAHAL

Glorious white dome, hanging in the sky
Four toy towers standing in an aether dream
Flowers writhing over the blurp marble arch
    "every 20 minutes (years) in Germany a
        whole mass movement of pricks" —
Heck — but the Taj Mahal forc'd
    a tear at the steps, looking out
        across the shrinking perspective
        green lawn
    To the perfect balance flower to flower
    (perspective is a shrinking of distance)
    the length of the lawn and mirrored
        trees on opposite
lawns facing the pool straight to the
        small square black door
on a vast marble surface where
    a man's an inch high upside down
beside a solitary marble tower at the
        edge of the white slabbed table
    Whereon sat the vast white dome
        in perfect stillness
    Whirling slowly round the sky-
        shine lotuspetal-seated cone peak
        gilded trident aloft,
    the eaglehawk slow circling in
        dusk rose light
the sun below trees dark green leaf-shoulders

    Arabesque bordered
archway parting the mystery
    in two symmetrical halves, —
split from blue sky-fork's gold point

141

thru the vast bulge of the soft dome
thru the dotted iron fountains arrowing
          down the blue-stained pool
          to the little black door
on the vast square chess-piece mounted white
          floor running with straight lines to the four towers
     blinking with creamy squares smaller up to stilted cupolas
     pasted on the flat surface of blue sky

Great invisible X's in pregnant space
          brain crossed into marble screens
     flowered dancing round the arch-point
in the Squared portal, mounted by dome-capped twin cupolas
     beneath the single circle white onion-eyehead
               floating marble moon-planet
standing 400 years over the Jamuna river
     stained only by the sun,
Bathed by the floor of mist at sun-crack,
as the eye travels round the diminishing
          huge dome
headed in every direction in straight
          lines from spire to spire
diminishing squares and expanding
          Domes cannonballed at 3rd eye
     Stereoptikon stroboscopic Stereophonic
          Silence-foreheaded soft white
               giant Thing of Hammered Marble
          Set everywhere with green gem-leaf
     & orange poppy budded flat flowers
                    — — —
a dog is barking
                    petal-flower
                              Parrots on the arches
the center is gone
                    the Rickshawcycle in the dark rupee
                         * * *
What we did — To Taj Mahal, stayed 2 Nites

142

Xmas even, raw Microphone Urdu voices
in neon blue at the Door — we slept
cold on a window ledge —
dry but inside warm alcove marble —
screened from the Door light
colorless dark gloom —
the sounds reechoing round
& round the balled church roof
resounding metallic or Stonelike
coined echo-vibration OM!
000's become louder in the
center of a Stone Hollow —
Great waves of sound frothing out of the arch
Voices echoed thru the green garden
           * * *
O Glorious bulge, marble filled with eyes,
balloon moving the sky apart
Help whistle the trees in your path

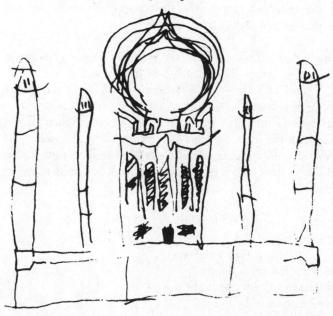

from the mouth of a Moghul moonbeam
O Spoken with Stone!   O Socialist Architecture!
With a golden bridge, or silver hanging
              in Full moon October's river
    Parted to the Black Taj imagined shiny marvel
         studded with Diamonds aloft
    Polished black marble reflecting starlight
Shajahan saw from behind this
              marble screen 2 miles away
                   from a tower in red Fort.

*Mathura New Year's Eve 196- —*

I have forgotten — the exact year-end'd name — Tracing backward thru registration & visa & passport numbers and dates —
    Walking thru Mathura's long streets — a puppy with muddy
back legs folded under behind, tail dragging on road sniffing
pavestones & water gullies — awkward steps of the front paws
pulling the collapsed rear of the little puppy — whom we fed
milk & nuts — in a leaf stitched cup —

    "I just had to tell somebody, I see visions of those girls raped
& left naked bound to lie in death on Chicago snow."
    New Years Eve 1956 — 1950 where was I? Last year on the
red Sea? or Massawa?
    What year is this that we have survived, triumphed, flour-
ished sat with the burning dead & slept on the warm marble of
Taj Mahal in misty nights with blankets — walked thru Fathe-
pur Sikri's palaces at night, under Orion & moonless Indian
December,

Tonite on the riverbank "Krishna
         Krishna"
                   May I see Krishna
    Please let me see Krishna
Behind latticework by flashlight the
         painted marble

144

Face with wide open eyes & arched eyebrow & charioteer's
        Mustache chauffeur with measles
    & flowers in his hair & beard in his teeth, sweet candy in the
stone bull's lips —
    inside the grillwork screen, yellow bulb gleam.
    Outside the white top of the wall against the sand & the
river, and twin lights across Jamuna, might be strong rose
stars —
        Where's
            The death of the NY Post
        in the soft rosy radiance of
            Krishna's new bridge on
                    the darkness, with store lights
                        in the middle —
            voices of radio on water
                    whispering down the ear —
        Calcutta, after it joins the
                            thick Ganga —
Krishna's river under the stars definitely
        "Shall we see Krishna?
                    and kiss Krishna's forehead
                        & lips?"
On the Lingam the man's pointed head
        gazing out, stony presence —
Joy to you & your cow — and the
black long reptiles sporting round
your neck — and yr. brother Shiva!

I didn't see Krishna I saw
        Krishnashiva by the river
    at night in garden, Jamuna garden
    in Mathura
                by candlelight —
    crosslegged filled with cigarette
        smoke & warm
    in silk shirt on the huge
    floor white cotton mattress inch —

145

Penahand & book on pillow
back in aether dreams of India —
Ganja or Morphine & sleeping pills — ,
Sitting crosslegged together
mind racing off into parties in Faraway
Manhattan — chancing on dark
oceans & Africa — red seas —
Killamanjaro, Place Rimbaud,
Kenyatta orating in Stadium I & Peter the lone whites sitting on
the grass —
Bounced out of Mboyas Wedding feast for not wearing ties &
Jackets —
in the marvelous Nairobi heat — cool nights near the movies
turning a corner from Indian restaurant —
a big square we walked, saw doctor for germs —
or the study of logistics, or Cosmic Paranoia —
the inhumans talking over Microphone Consciousness —
They got Elise? — She's where the dead are that went to the
burning ghats
or suffered "Chinese brutality" in the Himalayas —
Rishikesh & the naked Sages of Hardwar,
Marching on Ganja to Ganga
to bathe the fat man, Naga King or
Naga-guru —
Peter's big long year of hair — my own black locks & beard —
in mirrors shaded by candlelight
& yellow.
I once looked like that in a photo:
said Crabtree "Then you are that at least once in
Eternity" —
at least once in the random combination of happenings come
glimpses of recurrences, whether be dreaming of old friends
vanished by taxicabs, swept up into sky planes —
over London
or Maybe in Moscow — Such poetry as has seen the light —
The candle and a dog barking at the gate in the peacocked
park — Landing across the river, I bought picture of the gods

146

& demons at the bead or bidi-shopped facade of Venerable Bede
— a street in Mathura with all walkers and oxcart or pony horse
carriage — a private & clean blue Tonga, with the keys to the
mansion cottage south of town, on the river —

                    Asi ghat in Varanasi —
          quiet high walled alleys & white
          lights that end of town —

     Corpses at Hareschandra ghat, the
               striped tower — ducks quacking
                    at swanlings in the Paranoiac's
                              Bamboo playpen —
     Wanted by the Police!   Ray Bremser
     Wonder what's happening to him now Please dear Leroi —
     Reading the newspapers — how much gold is hoarded up
          in Crores —
     It's expensive to buy little silver Ganeshes —
     One of the candles just went out, another hollow candle —
     The year — ends with the same minute as remembers scat-
          tered fragments of the year —
     and Xmas at Taj Majal, dawn behind the marble screens —
     cold mornings, towers looking on the white marble sunshine —
     The arched shadows slowly moving to the center at midday —
     portals face the Sun exactly at noon —

     Here Krishna give me your hand to Joy in that Mortal beauty
          Till the pain comes that kills me Makes me change my
     mind's mind,
          to something mindless, that remembers its own starred logic
     less.
          A statue of Krishna, & wrapped in wool blanket my legs
     trembled to see so many stars & walk in the giant garden,
          The head of the witchcraft cult was captured in Sto.
     Domingo —
          The Thames is frozen over, first time in 15 years — Rhadas-
     wami's mausoleum with funereal botanic flowers all marble —

                              147

Puri & the bowed presence before Lord Jagganath
clomb to the lotus crest of Konarak's black alp-chariot
covered with Vishwamitra's cock —
Elura's walls — The Ravenna like octopus shaking undersea
deep thrones —
Mahakala the great skeleton — veined venereal Adam, Lord
of Death —
Kali the goddess of Nimtallah Street in her red cloth
Castro visit New York some freakish New Year present
Long space looking inward with eyes closed questioning who
am I? On the nod — a long circular horn or tram whistle echoing
around the high dome —
heard thru the forest on the walled riverbank — by the
water pump with watchman's candle lit — My own sputters &
I nod, & might now end.
Drowsy Salisbury S.A. Rhodesia London the head ganging
down the gangplank into the rural manpower plan
Salute sweet sixty one, two, three — "Gee I'll never forget
this new year's nite" — "Think I'll grow senile"
as the years advance and, my head balding, shrink like a
Junky's senile nose — like Tschombe in Katanga, or Lumumba
in hashish heat of death
Sail on O Mind, wherever you aim — All negroes can't be
great people — He wants to destroy Katanga, all the economic
stuff — away from the Newspapers
on the back in Jamuna.

It must be almost 12 now, & I'm too lazy to see this here
scribble to the stroke of midnite — have no watch — "Sick
Jokes" — the Universe no worse than a Jules Pfeiffer cartoon —
Gad what's he doin tonite?   and Neal in what garage strad-
dling tires?   J. gone to a big party at L.'s —
B. got my letter, all's well in Paris — Gregory cheerful by
mail & sniffing old sick-heart
My father lifts his glass of champagne to the TV set in quiet
winter — Snow probably all over East 34th and car wheels in
snowdrifts or granular ice prasad on asphalt —

Vishwinath Ghat — crude paintings of the child Demon-
killer — The Raksha's head cut off, and Krishna lifted a mountain to ward off dying Indra's tormented rains —
    Namaste, Worm I seek in the burning ghats, under the
bridge, in pilgrims stone cellars, by wood fires,
        Saddhus naked and bearded,
   clapping hand cymbal-blocks tinsel sound

of Hare Krishna Hare Ram Jai Cita Ram Jai Rhadakrishna —
                                        Jai '62
*Jan 2-3 — Mathura —*

Walking by Yamuna under concrete bridge — the burning ghat
in the sand with large parties of cardplayfellows in circles on
beach —
    Bungali ghat, the huge floppy bellied Govinda Kobi — (Krish-
na poet), hereditary Panda of riverside temple — with shastric
poetry rules & womanish silly smile, his "disciple" with mustached Turkish face & imaginative English — who gave me
their inscribed picture & a glass of bhang on the temple-house
roof under a tree with the broad river running by & huge sand
shore across the way.
    Living in abandoned summerhouse in Jamunabagh (garden)
— peacocks on the lawn & men & women walking along paths
shouting to keep away monkeys & ravens & parrots from the
mango trees — carrying double stringed bows to fling balls of
clay.
    Vultures tearing at a donkey body white soft mess in water
below Taj Mahal — dog intruding, up to belly in water, chasing
away the vultures —

*7 Jan 1963 —*

Dream — Midnite — A swimming pool & hotel corridor leading
to the U.S. White House — I am invited to visit but my dress
too scratchy & beat to go in — Jacqueline Kennedy comes along
very sweet & pretty & explains to me & can't be taken in White

House but would I like to come in to her sister's house next door?
I wake & feel ashamed.

Morning a huge ocean liner house we visit. Leo Skir has a job
working there, it turns out to be a big automaton ship with
sliding panels, greaseless purring huge white dynamos, passage-
ways that open & shut with electric eye — he works on the
ship & finds there's no one else there — a very eerie feeling —
I visit him to see the awful wonder of it — down the side of a
familiar railroad embankment to a huge factory run on the same
silent mysterious principle — as if the factory itself were a
living creature needing the attention of humans occasionally —

Peter Lawford's mother is with us — we are reading Kerouac's
huge book — great yellow leafs of poetry of one & 2 words per
line

> as you
> go sailing
> up yr
> mothers red
> ass to heaven
> send me a
> kiss wrapped
> in bandages
> I can shut
> my eyes to die with.

Admiring that, with Kennedy's sister or
whoever, an old republican lady, a matron from Florida presently
visiting Tanger —

her son goes off to purchase her a special highway machine —
not satisfied with local rickshaws, since he's Lawrence of Arabia,
he races down to the Fez or Marrakesh Desert to pick up a Sand
Dune Cycle for her, a better model —

wake up, & as I slowly remember fragments of the giant ship
& the factory with no windows & the awesome mystery rains in
my heart — reminds me of the unexplored depths of feeling all
man has — "moving around in worlds not realized — blank
misgivings."

Dream of Cary Grant — secret spiritual agent — film ghost
*Benares Wise Men*
Amulya Chakravaty — Vita Milk Factory — Samaren Roy's
Friend Achyut Patwarden — Krishnamurti Ashram (Foundation
for New Education, Raj Ghat)
Alice Boner — Assi Ghat

\* \* \*

*At Manikarnika Ghat:   Kashi*
Shambu Bharti Baba — Silent Naga, (whose photo I took) friend
of
Sri Mahant Ganga Giri — (guru of Sri Prabhakar Bramachari)
                         (of Nimtalla Ghat) Lives at Lahed
                         (or Lahad) Bhairat Mandir near Ali-
                         gura (never met) (says above Sham-
                         bu Bharti Baba)
*Holymen Benares:*
Kali Pada Guha Roy — family man — 14/7 Manasarovar 1st
flight above Kedar Ghat P.O.
     (Speak to Dabu Bannerjee   Phone 3807)
     Saturday 9 AM 22 December, 1962
                    For spiritual questions replied & possi-
                    ble Mantra (Diksha)
Kutta Baba — Bonpurwa Village (backside of University) —
          never met, Great Yoga (broken peasant Hindi)
Maha Moho   Padhyia Gopinath Kaviraj
               Lives near Maldahaya (near Benares Cantonment
               Station — 3 furlongs) called *Vesuda*
               *Ashram*
     Got these names from Naganand Muktikanth, student.

*January 12, '63 Benares*

There are certain limits — you can't push
     the cells of the Liver and
          brain become gigantic,

Transparent — diatoms
exploding —
et le printemps m'a apporté le rire affreux
de l'idiot
My kingdom is *not* of this world
Render unto Caesar

Till I have built Jerusalem
in England's green and pleasant land.

Unless the flesh die
on the cross
Chaitanya's arms upraised, palms outward
the little yellow painted wooden statue
waving over the door —
Upward — backed by the waving shadow
In the opposite direction from what
you thought, angel
Transcendency requires — your dread
of being torn apart
drifting between the spaces of the universe
out of Control — the car turning over
crashing around your head —
that's all, — orange shirt, red dishcloth,
red loincloth,
flesh hands writing —
Vishnu's many pink arms rotating
holding axes and flowers
Standing on an orange lotus
a red plastic begging bowl —
head spewing fire.
Blake's white life mask eyes are closed.
The wall deep in the mirror — What's in
the mirror, is it real?
Is the real room real?
I am lying on my shoulderblades
head up in the room, looking around

like a turtle from the mattress floor.

Towels draped hanging red from
    the black (wall cabinet) door.
Dogs barking streets away, a radio conversing
Farther and farther away — in love with
    His creation
Whose? who's He who closes his eyes?
Who's he who lies on his side with
    long yellow hair and breathes sleep?
Fear death — yet broken past the organic shell —
    What light outside of life?

Is He inside or out of this Mass
    of Images.

*Jan 13 —*

The complete fire is death.
    Not to sup with Landor Donne
    but see the eyes of Blake.
Blake my Guru.

The four different visions — ending, as I invoked the Spirit, at night walking around the Path in front of the New Library at 116 Street Columbia — ending with a crawling sensation, horror in my skull & the sky black closing down on me — uncanny & horrible apparition of — what — of — nothing describable in specific: A feeling, which was sudden, relating to the black crawling appearance of the sky — the sky the farther Universe itself — yet there was nothing apparent physical crawling in the sky. But the sensation of a living presence — Uncanny, — a non-human, implacably alien presence — to eat me up — then & there — Similar this 1948 vision to Ayahuasca horrors in Peru the night of the falling star & the God-blob.

Since this the last Sign from Blake or whatever might be named of that 1948 time — Perhaps schematized to indicate the limits of human perception — beyond that — bordering off into

153

the non human — If you want to see *that* — It's serious — maybe death — naturally — being beyond the nature of mental flesh perception — thus perhaps telling me — "a sign" — to shut up & live in the present temporary form — that's all that form can be, what it at present is — till it literally dies. After that it's another matter, incomprehensible to that which comprehends flesh universe only — flesh a bad word — Body —

*Benares* —

Walk this afternoon along ghats, the beauty of the crowded bathing nakedness, buffaloes washed by thin loinclothed trainer — Manikarnika ghat again after several weeks — a detached head of a fourtyish man — burning, some red juices dribbling out nose or eye, down cheek, dropping off bright red hot ear — scalp split & cream color skull still smooth & dry in the heat peeping thru the blackened hair — and further on in another pyre a chunk of rubbery blackened meat & bone a foot long, the last of the body (probably backbone & thigh?) pushed by poles — a peter-pan nymph in brown rags cooking her liquids in a can in the white ashes of an abandoned pit — stirring the ashes around the can with a stick — barefoot — seen her before — I looked to see if her breasts were covered — yes with a square of burlap hung from one shoulder.

Dream — Several nites ago huge figure of Swami Satyananda's 2 thumbs.

*Jan 17, 1963* —

Tonite — with a witch woman, the cleaning lady, a secret saddhu — I am in her apartment — sitting on her back — she says, you want me to do a good job, come back later today when I'm finished with my work — cleaning up — I get off her back (she'd been outstretched prone, I'd been sitting on her — at a window) — perhaps she'd been washing the floor — a thin hag — like the Sweeper in this house to whom I gave a rupee & she bowed hands folded at breast to me yesterday — So I say I will

154

come back later to the Dream lady Guru — When I return after a daylong dream absence — she's there, ready & prepared to go to her home — to go to work with me, she's put on a fur hat — to go out — and says by hall closet, "You wanted to know if there are any other real experts — Well by good chance, one of the best saddhahs around came today" — out of the closet or bathroom walks a tall red robed figure — large man in heavy tibetan robes — with seemingly no head but held by his hand a small bright hole where his head should be — he's holding by hand up there a telescope

which, when he takes away from before his face, I see a large rugged handsome face (later, writing, I realize it's Brian Gysin) — A feeling of pleasure in the dream.

Waking, my resentment at Gysin goes away — I must have been jealous.

* * *

Walking home thru dark alleys from the burning ghat where we sat & chatted with Shambu Bharti Baba saddhu (who'd taken vow silence 4 years ago since he "had nothing good to say") — it being tonite eve of Saraswati Puja (devotional festival to Goddess of Music Poetry & Scholarship) — nearing our door, we saw fireworks up the street & stayed to watch an odd procession

— for a wedding or for Saraswati — a band of snake pipe players, a band of drummers & bagpipers, a lighted float showing a
map of India with Nehru's face in the lights fed by a loudly
whirring motor trailing in a big trycicle, followed by two elephants with small crowds of riders aloft! then a string of camels
padded past in slow motion, and a series of paper mache or clay
images — first a red big-trunked big pink eared Ganesh, then
Shiv & Parvati sitting on a small mountain balanced by an old
lady on her head, then various other godly figures, then a team
of horses pulling an empty carriage crowned with electric lights
— and a man in a palanquin with head bowed as his feathered
golden turban was too high for the low box roof he sat under —
as the parade came down Desaswamedh St. there cows stam-
peded running down the empty street toward the steps down to
the dark river in mist — frightened by huge red sparklers that
advanced before the pipe & drum noises — the Elephants went
down a side alley — stepping cautiously aside from the grey-
beard blind beggar who sits in the street all day & sleeps in his
same spot all night — Peter & I followed the huge high ass of
the elephant into the narrow alley — it loomed ahead of us
blocking the brightness of the streetlight with its bulk & making
a big round elephant ass wall moving between the houses stone
sides up the olden passageway, turning the narrow corner near
a Shiva altar — where the elephants stopped & hesitated while
the drivers consulted whether to turn back or get deeper into
the noisy bright lit parade filled Bengali Tola (alley) opening up
ahead, when the marriage house glared with midnite sitters &
loudspeakers played noisy movie songs from housetop corners.

* * *

A Natural Poetry — the problem is to write Poetry which is,
which *sounds* natural, not self conscious.

Generally rhymed verse sounds self conscious — except
where some Genius has opened up & the Self Consciousness is
lost in a burst of sincerity or passion or amazement or ecstacy,
or comedy, — as in Hart Crane —

156

By Self Consciousness, meant here simple "sophomoric" recognizable egotistic self consciousness — most minor academic verse that passes for high professional style is like that — Not to be confused with awareness of process of language — for instance Yvor Winters verse sounds self conscious, the professional awareness of the tone is a tone an attitude, is annoying despite the kind of intelligence applied — Not natural to the man in the man — merely a "stance" — favorite word for many self conscious minor poets. The "depth" there is not natural, it's synthetic etc.

*Jan 20 —*

Sleeping lately on top of my dreams too many hours to remember. Last nite, fucking a small dollike baby girl — almost had wet dream woke with tide-surge of sex reaching to the tip of my penis in my underwear as lay beside Peter on the mattress floor. Woke but didn't come — remember fucking down into the little doll girl hole with many people watching, like at a turkish bath.

Jan 28, 1963 —
Dismal America

## SARASWATI'S BIRTHDAY

Jai Guru Jai Sarawati
at the altar in the white room
    Prasad in leaf cups
        orange slice, cherry-yellow, milk sweets,
           hard sweet rice, Guava Slices,
The carpeted roof top
    Squatters & Sitters leaning
        into the wavy music
    under the orange canopy
        by the night trees Ganges
           waterfront street

Springtime's fifth day —
    The — quavering voices of the
        young singers in blue jackets
    leaning together groaning out of
        chest & belly
    ohohoheaoh — oo oo — Jai Guru
Flowers resting yellow and green
    buds over the flat fields
    The Saddhu's tree trunk altar
        creation cock with flowers
    mouthfuls of pea buds
        green softness of taste
    sweet saliva —
Mustard plants & wheat ripening
Across the river from Ramnagar
    by slow poled boat
on blue seeming water —
    Skeletal boatman turbaned
        on head & loins
    hollow armed

158

one anna received at the shore stall
        under the umbrella, sleek lazy
    Man-concessionaire acceptant
            of the angry coin —
    Eee Eeee — Ee Ee Ee —

Coming down the stairs
step by
step down —
Trilochan's pants
seen down
thru
the doorway
the doorway
to the street —

a continuous descent thru miles of space
floating freely                    rising
after awhile        and

f
a
l
l ing under comp le te   control ∿∿∿   like

walking across a tightrope high over

_____

oooooooooooooooooooooooooooooooooooooooooooooooooooooooooooooo

millions of spaceships or planets in the extremest
spaces — the black void itself —
filled with solid objects —

164

Stars flying away — never to
        be reached
    unless you screw up Time
            itself —
a happy night of Saraswati's birthday
            Goddess of learning
        Queen of Sanskrit prosody
Music over the roof —
                (bodies burning on the levels
                    of Manikarnika ghat
                    under the head of the Smoking tower —
        looking down into the Bosch-flares of
                    winter sick & Springtime dead
            — a procession of four crying *Ram's Truth*
                carrying the two foot thin corpse
                stiff in colored silk —

Blake on the wall last week,
        eyes closed frowning on my
                insults to the Professor
I skipped in the room ashamed & fluttered
        my face with my fingers —
Tonite the white mask face eyes now closed
        to listen to the music with a
                faint smile
    of wonder at the Perfection
            Bullshit Singing
            patted with tablas, droning harmonium,
                voice skipping after midnight
                its ni ni ni's of Minnie Springtime
    Paganini-staged in Advance
    by the great Slap of Creation
Wherever it happened & wherever it's
        going it's here right now —

                    * * *

"lacking in substantiality"

165

Rather Say: The wind is playing
        with the lady's skirts
              under the Magnolia trees
        where the Artful police prepare
              My Mistress Muse's Downfall
                    Chattanooga, Montgomery, New Orleans —
Springtime in February in Benares
              first consciously realized in Words —
        long walk on the hard mud-stept bank
              by the fields —
The sun like an orange streak of Jetplane
                    fire exhaust bolting
                          across the flat topped
                                river rippling motionless

                    Must've been passing water at
                          the time —

*Feb 2 Evening* —

All that happens about everything
from the transistor radio backward
down the black stair hole, fingers to the wall
        eyes closed on the corners
        stepped in from the street
        The beggar sleeping on my steps
        the path back over the sand bank
              steps at water's edge
        Lights silvering and red on the
                    grey waters —

        Half moon at darkfall
        the Stars!   the black-blue vastness
              brightened with white stars
        Hail the inimit spacyness of
              cold blueity there outside
                    my eyeglasses

166

including my spaceless soul —
that acts thru
sex like thru an eyeball

Coughing on the steps crouched
under the burning court —
Smoke rising in my downward stare
on another red flamey bed —
with the Big red bellied Elephant
Sitting naked on a big pillow
His mousey devotee a black
Rat like myself
Praying for his Incarnate Inspiration
to deliver the word
confounding Asuras
Swallowing all in his black
Stomach
or granting them powers
to overcome Illusion, Jynkx,
& Poverty
with Elephant Eyes
Impersonally perched in his
large narrow red head
and big white ears
listening to Faraway tents filled
with Images of Krishna, & shouting
devotees with a drum and
Microphone Sleep
eyes closed,
dreaming of worship shirted
voices
My foot slipped in mud,
I smoked a bidi followed the trip
backward from the footsteps up &
down in the dark
feeling the wall —
of the crys and curbstone for shit

of the blind beggarwoman wrapped
    in her mattress on the steps
      of the cloth Merchant —
passed by unseen giant elephants
    stepping aside her bundle tent
The voices sing all night, all
    past 7 nites roaring the same

    Sri Ram Jai Ram Jai Jai Ram,
    Jai Ram Sri Ram Jai Jai Ram,
    Sri Ram Jai Ram Jai Jai Ram,
    Jai Ram Sri Ram Jai Jai Ram.
          \* \* \*
"He looks on his relatives as venemous snakes. . ."

*Dream Feb 4, 1963 —*

Afternoon — sleeping on mattress floor on stomach in dark afternoon night fall —

On a long street — I've recieved letter from Bill — Wandering to different restaurants from an earlier dream an old dim grey Greenwich Village — lost — I see huge plate glass window covered with paper (decorations) flowers and double door, that I recognise having been to before — once, in Mexico perhaps, like that of bare tabled restaurant upstairs I ate steak with Jack inside it — Mexico City — I push door open, to my relief it's busy inside, a bandstand & people at tables, waiters & bar men — I see also at a window table, one of the small side tables, Bill B. is sitting as usual alone eating — I see only dimly my eyes half closed in the dream — I ask "Is that really you, Bill" and he says "yes, I just flew back from Paris" — "But I just got a letter from you!" "Yes I didn't have time — one travels so fast these days — Special arrangement on the planes — just go to airfield & ask for ticket & your flight is arranged immediately, next plane out. Whereas if you advance reserve you have to fill out all sorts of papers & wait for weeks —" he gives a long complicated explanation which I can't follow tho I get the

general impression that he's circumvented the Flight bureau-
cracy — I am leaning forward talking to him, intimate at table
again. . . Scene changes I'm running down streets in India followed by a mob of devotees — I'm flying toward the river to
bathe, or else to see Bill again — one of the Indian guards takes
me by the hand and pulls me along even more swiftly, apart
from the pack of people — we approach a corner where the
street narrows — sudden intrusion of corner of building on the
sidewalk, so you have to run in the street, over a black muddy
cobblestoned alley — I'm running across this thinking "alas
that when I was young I didn't give myself completely to Bill
to love since he was my guru I should have let him fuck me
more, I should have made love to his body & sucked his cock as
he pleased instead of cutting him off & rejecting him like that"
— as thinking this my body's flying down the street in the
posture of ass up to be screwed — Peter comes in with Morphine
& I wake up.

*Dream Jan 10 — 4 AM —*

Trying to get back thru the railroad riverbed flood houseboats
to first home. On the Riverside I meet old stranger friend who
hails me from free associations before. I deny his acquaintance
and strike up a bargain. The shining green automobile starts off
by a twist of the red flesh knob.
  Sweating under the blankets. . waking to the sound of dripping tap water & pressure against bladder . . . in squat-john to
empty my body of water . . . Mme. Alexandra David Neel's
statement of principles of first perception similar to Huxley's
"reducing valve" simplification. Tibetan Buddist "Secret oral
Doctrines" — & "Visionary Experience" —
  If I dream & lay back & remember from the remembering —
scene backward or forward — it sometimes rearranges itself into
another dream & I drift off — or get my hand bitten by a mosquito on the page, lifeless.
  Here some vague recollection of the river — travelling the
river to get to — home —

169

I can go out there to Benares Hindu Univ. to visit this pie shaped church front stairs — behind which a statue of Buddha — anytime — whether invited or not —

*Jan 9, 1962 Benares (Visit from C.I.D.)*

The Policeman flew in the black door
      on wooden wings
I was sitting at a wooden table eating
      borsht and answering questions —
He was so polite he was making me feel
      like a pig Salesman's Convention —
Grunts & squeaks of Suspicion amid the
      bargaining for identity cards
He said he came as a friendly visit just
      to check up my existence
Sitting on my woven mats with his CID
      card dangling from his fingers,
Round faced, with a short Cezanne mustache
      under his nose, refusing
My offer of salad from Mother Moon's kitchen,
With the two German professors inquiring
      suspiciously of his legal approxamatively
      correct reasurances
Which led to letters mistyped & forgotten
      to the Superior Chief of Polices —
All because a 28 year old blond photog-
      rapher for Esquire
who made 35,000 a year, expenses paid
      by the Tourist Bureau
Trailing his three cameras and telephoto
      scope lenses
Sticking out hung from his rubber face
      Suddenly disappeared in broad
daylight on the ghat steps in the bright
      sunlight invisibly
Suspended in time like his camera snapping

the snout of Buffalo,
horns lifted at the shore, swift tongue
sliding snotfully to his large black nostril
    wet with Ganges —
Very satisfying the click of the instant as
    The Squire in slacks appeared
kneeling to click the beast delayed
    nose wipe touch inward
on the right ear of his inky-wet Moo-burp
    Sea-mucous tasting
    Smell hole —
Returning to the German posessor who
    disapproved unpaid expropriation
    in Ceylon — oil gaz stations, Esso etc.

Quite understood all according
    to the Landlord's flowry Shastra

*Jan 10, 1963 —*


While the black haired lady begger Kali Ma wrapped in a
mattress on the opposite corner at midnight talked to herself like
a rooster
    imagining the blind leper down the street was trying to steal
her tin cup before her opaque marble eyes —
    She only gets up on scratchy legs to totter to the curb to crap,
holding up her rags — Her husband left her there & someone
took care of her feet died —

And the police later apologized — the raw youth did a lousy job
    of revealing our Identity to the Dentist downstairs —
                              * * *
    Harinama Mantra

Hare Krishna, Hare Krishna
Krishna Krishna, Hare Hare
Hare Rama, Hare Rama

Rama, Rama, Hare Hare
    (16 Names in 32 letters Devanagri Script)

*Morphine Fragments 14 Feb 1963 —*

Moonlit Moslems walking past
the Taj Dome trees.

    — — —

    Moslems in the Moonlight,
        asphalt bomb!

    — — —

Moths & butterflies
        drifting above the Green bush
Whirling in sunlight — what for?

    — — —

    Heartfelt (Kaddish)

    — — —

Poetry a "picture" of consciousness
        Picture nix — paradigm?
I feel I'm fogetting something

    — — —

ROOM DROWSE MEDITATION

Blake Mask tacked on wall
Black photo life made plaster
Cricket chirps here & in Bunhill Field
Stone "Somewhere near this ground"
I have been waiting 15 years
all time thinking Harlem befutured
But heartfelt the minute of now
Postponed except for orange mist
flat mirror Ganges dusk boatfulls
Pipe laying thin Notes in Farness
I heard relaxing smoking cigarettes
pen balanced in hand on the nod
grey platforms concrete over the Steps
of Bather men with brown fat bellies

and Strings hanging ear to abdomen
Sadhus taking bearded constitutionals
Like Cony Island hot dog businesmen
"I have drifted from Harlem to the Ganges,
East River to Benares seeking Yourself
Whom I love in faith, hopelessly"
the long long roar of surrounding trains
arrived crawling like ants on across bridge
Delivering professors of Noise to the hot platform
Elephant scaled to cloth wrapped beg women
Seated on the laboratory stational floor —
Monotone years waiting for thee Traveller
faster than light or Sex abstraction
eating writing about that I Am
forever despite now I can't feel things —
I am a lost soul, a poor lost soul
like I always felt after I was told born —
on the Fair Street kissing Olive the girl
Who got lost when I moved up to Haledon —
I must have loved her because I dreamed
lostly visiting apartment stairways
& neighborhoods I could never find Marbles
in the earth squares by the telephone
building wall next to the Sidewalk
on the corner across from the Synagogue
I was scared of half a block down
from the RR. bridge overpass — silk
Factory, cardboard cone-spools
I looked for messenger jobs 20 years
later on the same street child Neighborhood
I couldnt find Olive — oh Olive if you read
this now, could you remember me kiss
our relationship, I didn't wear glasses
those days can you recognise at least
the street cement porch and dread drain holes
Upstairs in the kitchen Don Feitlowitz' family
table — years later the Morning Call life

173

I visited — my boyfriend who tickled armpits
on Broadway when I said pubic hair by Mistake —
that was nice a delirious surprise that someone
could tickle your armpits in broad daylight
I was a coward everyone discovered something
about Me forever that instant I got scared
to make believe I was indifferent, instead of
laying down on the Masonic Temple lawn
around the corner from the butcher and let me
be honestly thrilled for an hour like the Movies.
But who Cares in Benares It's a dead World
Say the Buddhists and someones vomiting
at dawn by the pump and clearing his kretched
throat O Milkstand of Now!  Even that's
not real, on my back on my Mattress Om
Cat pur, dog bark, retch-cough, drip
& groaning buzz of the train on the bridge
its whistle tweet tweet O alas I can't see
you invisible Olive, tho I can hear the
train still now & see a picture of Blake.
O Sounds!  O cigarette forgotten in clay ash
tray, spire of smoke, my eyelids heavy
I am as buzzing round the glary bulblight
a mite catches my eyeglasses and a Mouse
scratches in garbage spread paper below table
they think me aimless I do not know
why I am doing all that myself doth
thusly wording the catch of fish thought
all there is in my Ganga head with
eyes closed reopening on two months
this room full of Me & Peter scratching
his back and buttocks the Map of India
tall as a man I've got to get home to
Somewhere groaning in me or swiftly
forgotten time bells will pass sans
proper sincere notation except some yogi
seated blind drifts attention from

174

the words to hear their sound equal
in deep black mental space nowhere
except your periscope feet trip down
Measuring the "frame of reference" cow street
Spacyness which must be there, if I
can actually descend the black stairwell
downstairs to the place which is Dasaswamedh
Street called by Name, but quite solid
when you get there, if ever, as usual.

Writing about writing.   XX Cent Criticism
Should symbolize what happens when
writing turns inside out to write writing
after Gertrude Stein died about it.
Don't want to be cynical, just
the present morphined physiological
curtains of cellophane pierced by Mongrel
dog-barks — That night in bed with Hal
& Bill & Jack flirting on the 116 St floor —
on Benzedrine — Talking about transparent
waterfalls of cellophane — pure synthetic
abstraction making me groan with desire
to be kissed on the mouth & held close
to the breast of the fair boy's body I
desired then & there but it wasn't done
so I talked all night explaining my
delicate condition as hurt-voiced as I felt
in my crying throat & sad warm 18 yr. old breast —
Is my breast a sad warm thing as of yore,
right now?   only If I think of that & let it go
or grab Peter by the knee & kiss his thigh
I am a Masochist said the mental textbook
I always knew that, its the only love
I ever got — Nobody loves me, I'm old
ugly Allen Now like I dreamed I always
was when I was tender boy with hide-outs
rubbing my flesh tube down in my legs —

That came for the first time in Cony Island
or Revere Beach in the Shower-bathroom — using
a cardboard toilet paper inner tube for a yoni,
surprised when the heat that built up flashed out
at my groin with spurts of white wet fire
— I never caught on — a dwarf laugh forever
making things sound bad — I'm not complaining,
I just wonder how it all happened so fast
that now I'm almost Middle aged & got 3 grey hairs
That's not fair!   To whom else do you give
Money, if not to the Indian store at the foot
of the 42'd St Independent Subway Bookstore
Steps with Van Gogh prints huge
window — Something admirable about how
they buy pictures if you show them to the
untouchable street sweeper where he can see it —
I'm drifting away crosslegged into cigarette.

* * *

### Describe: The Rain On Dasaswamedh

Kali Ma tottering up steps to shelter tin roof, feeling her way to
> curb, around bicycle & around a leper seated on her way
> — to piss on a broom
left by the Stone Cutters who last night were shaking the street
> with Boom! of Stone blocks unloaded from truck
Forcing the blindman in his grey rags to retreat from his spot
> in the middle of the road where he sleeps & shakes under
> his blanket
Jai Ram all night telling his beads or sex on a burlap carpet
Past which cows donkeys dogs camels elephants marriage pro-
> cessions drummers tourists lepers and bathing devotees
step to the whine of serpent-pipes & roar of car motors around
> his black ears —
Today on balcony in shorts leaning on iron rail I watched the
> leper who sat hidden behind a bycicle
emerge dragging his buttocks on the grey rainy ground by the
> glove-bandaged stumps of hands,

176

one foot chopped off below knee, round stump-knob wrapped
with black rubber
pushing a tin can shiny size of his head with left hand (from
which only a thumb emerged from leprous swathings)
beside him, lifting it with both ragbound palms down the curb
into the puddled road,
balancing his body down next to the can & crawling forward
on his behind
trailing a heavy rag for seat, and leaving a path thru the street
wavering
like the Snail's slime track — imprint of his crawl on the muddy
asphalt market entrance — stopping
to drag his can along stubbornly konking on the paved surface
near the water pump —
Where a turban'd workman stared at him moving along — his
back humped with rags —
and inquired why didn't he put his can to wash in the pump
altarplace — and why go that way when free rice
Came from the alley back there by the river — As the leper
looked up & rested, conversing curiously, can by his side
approaching a puddle.
Kali had pissed standing up & then feeling her way back to the
Shop Steps on thin brown legs
her hands in the air — feeling with feet for her rag pile on the
stone step's wetness —
as a cow busied its mouth chewing her rags left wet on the
ground for five minutes digesting
Till the comb-&-hair-oil-booth keeper woke & chased her away
with a stick
Because a dog barked at a madman with dirty wild black hair
who rag round his midriff & water pot in hand
Stopped in midstreet turned round & gazed up at the balconies,
windows, shops, and city stagery filled with glum
activity
Shrugged & said *Jai Shankar!* to the imaginary audience of Me's,
While a white robed Baul Singer carrying his one stringed dried
pumpkin Guitar

177

Sat down near the cigarette stand and surveyed his new scene,
just arrived in the Holy City of Benares.
* * *
Prem I met at 4 AM by the milk stand — a conversation in
English "Bloody fool" etc educated in St. Pauls Church school
in Madhya Predesh —
"Ganja is the first step toward preparation for a sadhana" —
"I am a Saint without rules" —
Then met on ghats tonite — tea & chilam (pipe of ganja) he
singing & translating a song of Bacchan — version of Omar
K —


"When I die — My wife this is my instructions —
When I die — because I been drinking every day as far back
　　　as I can — lost my memory —
But if anybody wants to perform my Corpse Service
Don't put tulsi leafs on my mouth & pour on Ganges water
Sprinkle my mouth with country liquor instead
And wash my body in my own Ganges which is as you know
　　　Wine —
Nobody carry my corpse except a bunch of drunkards
Because even if one stumbles the others will roll on
And I'll go my usual unsteady way to the burning ghats —
And if anybody asks you who the corpse is
(While they're banging around the gulleys of Benares
Not crying Ram Nam Satahay but Country Likker Shop's the
　　　Truth)
and my Dharma and Mantra and Sadhana & my Caste —
Tell them I was by caste a big Drunkard, my Sadhana was
　　　pouring wine & being pourd,
Tell the truth my Path to stand at the bar counting my Rud-
　　　raksha beads
With each glass of Wine, crying *Tavern Tavern Tavern*
naming my God *Wine Wine Wine* 1000 times a day in a holy
　　　stupor."

So I asked, what kind of verse is that?

"Rubber Chand" — rubber lines — that's what Neerala wrote too — some critic called it rubber — because you can pull the lines out or snap them in short any way you got the strength. — Rubber Meters.

*Shivaratri 1963 Feb 22 — 11: A.M. — (Shiva's Birthday.)*

Last night across the Ganges over the black trees and river on the lit hill the gongs clanging
Lying on pneumatic plastic & wool blanket in bare room, with cigarettes & book
"I write with Electric speed" the pink domed man in afghan soft brown robe — Tottering helped the flesh bulk smiling "In your own heart Guru" — said Shivananda Change-Delight —
Three sadhus in a row under trees, one eyes transfixed & bloodshot open, one with a crush-jawed freaktooth Nandi cow chewing its twisted cud, — one smeared with ash across the river at Laxman Jula —
One year and many train nights awake; smoking in the bunk & reading Time atrocities in Viet Nam
Red boys handcuffed photograph by grassy river kneeling in whose army's U.S. eyed capturer can't remember detail enough 365 Newspapers of the year.

Early noon at the pavement above fires by the open steps into the pit yard
Passing with Peter thru Manikarnika, the old dark man I'd seen days earlier crouching in shadow curld up on Steps — fires &
Confusion? — Someone come waiting early to die —
Now as first time seen lying too near the fire — his hair white frizzy skull dry ashen high temples & yellow eyes open
Beckoning with kindling thin bony arms — the brown foot swollen & shiny — calling me — Down steps — he opened his eyes & said Panni! He? Panni — and a clay ashen cup at his head —
Legs now stretched out hollow no muscles long Buchenwald

179

skeletal legs & no cheek but a bone, flat pelvis under the white thick loincloth in the grey ashes —

a burn-sore on the right ankle — flies festering on wound & near eyelid —

Eyes closed — flitting by eyebrow, eared big in dry grey ash-head — delicate large starved bony nose —

inexpressable grey in the holes of transparent Who looks in, out of these eyeballs — rheumy

mouth open the large grinning teeth of Skeleton — "Panny" with dry bright red living tongue —

I washed cup at the lower step & brought large mouthful — he lifted his arm birdcrane hand with the red brickcolor teacup

— Peter standing above holding butter & milk can in Israeli net bag —

Pour water into his deep mouth — "My sadhana was pouring wine & being poured"

and then beckoned me nearer in Hindi To Ask —

What I could not garble from between his teeth & gentle tired wave of his long arm —

I went & up Steps past tree, found basket of yellow curry potatos — left

Wrong hysterical leaf plate of potatos in the ash-step near his head — a cow's brown nose

waved aside by that rake-handle arm — He didn't eat.


Later bathing near the fires on steps surrounded by boats I pushed & hung my head under the prow in deep water,

Washed underwear on wet steps with red soap — my hair scrubbed & cracks of feet & ears in red loincloth —

Climbed up to where the Naked Man I'd saluted earlier — by his holiday fire with shrivelled soft ashey cock lap — resting between legs — hand held up in

Soft reassurance Shambu Bharti Baba sat — some wheaten pancake & peas in ghee & potato leaf mouthfuls — a pipe passed with the university employee

in white underwear — who greeted me on the mat "you have just come from your bath?" — seated crosslegged with loincloth hanging on iron pipe —

"That man I didn't understand his ashey Hindi idea, could
we ask why he was dying?"
How long & what need I couldn't tell — except potatos —
tho now as we went down, a clay cup of milk
half emptied near his face — Leaning over seeing his weak
knobs & under his garment
the sharp shrunken flesh hung on hairy bonewracks — "To
be taken down — to the water — too hot up here" —
Flies buzzing on his forehead in the bright sunlight glaring
over his forehead's deep bridge —
over the burning ghats — carried under the sky my hand at
his inner knee & wooden backbone — head hanging carried by
the arms my companion
"Said he's wants to cold, hot, river down leave" —
Down to the river on a step, weak & foot hanging over step
then pelvis slipping down next step near water — we lifted him
up after
inquiring of the Skullhead which fainted & woke at once
looking up with
its eyes at ours blandly — Been there 2 weeks I seen him before at night by high coals arm raised to protect his forehead
eyes held weightless bar —
Some extreme Sadhu? Just come here to die — who was he?
— We left him there
& went on to Scindia gate thru temples & Darshans of Shiva-
gi's father's temple — looking out of the high castle balcony —
Down the river in the clear blue air clean after last nite black
rain —
We'd seen, walking before — by the crowded Sky Crow-
vultures wheeling over the Mosqued Embankment — in the
water the white decaying cow afloat, sat on by birds & plucked
bobbing in the slow flood — drift & forget — $ — vultures
flagging the sky now for that same Cow whose head twisted
back tied to the shoulder thru mouth
Slung on two poles front & back & five loinclothed workmen
in the midnite sludging down the steps bearing the felt-grey
bloat-weight of the stomach pregnant with white mouths —

Untied & slumped footward to the water
on a shelf head hung back waiting for the sleeping boatman
of cows —
peeped from a tower next afternoon the waves of blackflap
meatbirds —

Arrived at Bursar's mandir cow-shed — drawings in white &
bright red powder Swastika on the
damp cow smell stone — a small peaked whitewashed altar
under the cell
roof, huge stone bowls in the corner on blocks — a perch
halfway up the wall by window into great chanting temple and
closer a stone cluttered, walled, private two-yard nook —
playing with babe while cows ate straw-water mush & old
Brahmin chanted & flattered the cow-neck dewlap with mantric
hand —
Inside the large temple, songs of Sankar — Sanskrit choruses
& answer-question word calls —
His daughter by the door, his tea we sat at stall porch over
street — I back walking thinks past Manikarnika —

Greeted by Chandal the pole-man who'd given him — as he
lay on humid puny ground four steps away from flower-ashy
brown water —
"——" a tobacco — one Chandal rubbed it in his palm — &
dropped the few grains between
the skeleton's teeth who smiled upside down I'd seen him
close his cheooooth & mum mouth the bitterness grains
Now he's here I am pointed he lies close-eyed stretched on the
bottom step foot swollen in the shallow lapping purple dreep —
Head resting on top white step in its grey frizzy skull flies on
the dead sore & eyelids mucus closed — silent — still —
The chandal pointed to heaven — "Haribol!"
Namaste at the figure — I sauntered to see close his quiet thin
body at rest — instant gone — Who now & where? —
Burn & scatter ash in Ganges to be — all day the cries of Jai
Ram & Jai Shankar — & Primititti tu ta primititti tu ta too in
the afternoon silence of stone

182

Kali-Ma made of papier-mâché, Bengal

Rembrandtean beggar by Deshbandu Park, Dasawamedh Ghat, Benares

Shambu Bharti Baba, December 18, 1962

Shambu Bharti Baba, December 18, 1962

Kali-Ma (see the poem *Describe: The Rain on the Dasawamedh*, p. 176)

Leper beggar-boy, Dasawamedh Ghat, Benares

Peter Orlovsky lying dressed in pants on mattress with long
Hollywood Christlike hair & Christ's small beard, Benares

One dog walks on 3 legs, the left back leg retracted . . . (see p. 138)

Monkeys visiting rooftop of Brahmin's house wherein Ginsberg and Orlovsky lived for six months above a sacred alleyway down to Dasawamedh Ghat bathing steps peopled by beggars pilgrims Sadhus & wandering cows, Benares, December 19, 1962

Householders wrapped in shawls carrying brass waterpots trudging into the Ganges steps, passing & observing the beggar-men (see p. 130)

A lady arrived with small baskets of parsley & radishes sits in the
road where it turns down to the river (see p. 133)

shelf — the sun still bright on the body stretched over the steps down to the river — woeless loinclothed — Had he eaten those potatoes & drunk those milk before me and tasted already the ashy apple of What?

Away! away! over the roofs, over the sky into the dark clouds — into the rolling creation that ship sailing on surrounded by

Ganges Waters in India, close down to the houses & towers the frontage & red peaked temples, the buffaloes quietly standing over the path — the pea-drains asmell in the wet earthgullies —

a skull in the flames later an eyebrow I didn't see burn — only large fires & beating of black meat by the thudding pole — collapse of legged log-char chunks —

& Jai Shankar for the afternoon left — for the thousand eyes searching & mouths

crying Jai Ram Jai Shankar Jai Shiv for tonight in their imaginary bed

Shiv god of Meditation and Blackness with his snake chains & bracelets & mount-piled hair with dear Ganges faucet

pouring from his high locks set with the mooncrescent —

Shiv whispered in his very ear today — and was listening in all ears as he entered

the last sound Jai Narayan! in that black holey place amid crackling

wood — Same man I saw dying before & before & before — nights walking lonely past his lone skeleton curled up, knee bent at fire — and feeble head & arm that waved at a cow an hour before protecting his bitter

last potatoes — all the Singers at once, calling on the God Shiva the god Ram —

Jai Jai Victory to whoever he is Now — as Ezra Pound may be — cut off your head, Kabir —

We all under Kali's foot or in Shiva's Bhang or Chillam high ganja reverie foreboding & dry mouth

the last I saw of — Spoken to him his last day, his last hours — sang in a temple whilst he sang in his own —

"And my grandmother's head exploded — bathed her and

cleaned and then burned — directly to heaven it comes out thru the top of the skull — "

It's the same old story of Kurt Shwitters playing politics with Marinetti —

Primititti — And Poetry as a Sadhana —

But to have faith in Who? and love who? & weep for who but all us Whos alive — a *great* dream by the ghats walking home and a tear for my Mentor

who taught so peacefully patient with his thighless leg skin —

And still ringing in the loudspeaker by the temple top covered to the shoulder by sand, hung with flowers tent & loudspeaker & Naga Sadhu with rope waist & long thin hair — praying hellow! on the giant telephone — Who told him the numbers of the fires? The

glasses of bhang on my blanket mattress seat surrounded with books & bottles of bhang & the professors of Walt Whitman lost in Northern India Patrika the rest of the War-news & photographs of soft tits of Playboy — and the secret oral teachings in Tibetan Boodhist Sects —

"ostentation continues in time of crisis" — Coughing in the alleys at Dasaswamedh — a dog barks by the Milk Stand — Crickets & Ram name & snores in the wooden Silence —

"after the first death" reassures Thomas — "there is no other" — "He's gone & the ship

Sails on forever No one knows where the Whole wandering Dutchman Universe —

To be returned to Sender if Not delivered — that Kali Yuga come & Ghandi perhaps an

avatar creating in the Chaos his rules no vegetables & nakedness locomotives & Guru Ghokale —

*Aether* flying thru *Quest* —

The quiet at the end of the year — the Second Shivaratri, the night streets calm & eerie,

No much man about — as I went home to Peter's needle Krishna drowse & cold leftover sips of Bhang & gentle milk —

Newspaper & cigarettes, taxation & sentiment, arguments between bidi sellers & clothesrobbers, slap on old & young —

184

Earlier at Magh Mela in Prerag a clonk on the head & Sadhu
plonked down crying for his Mamma's Bhog — holymen fight-
ing!

"the Kohinoor no great thing on the toe
    of Mumtaz Mahal,"
the Taj not doubled in the glassy postcard
    pond upside down mineature
image in the deathcell wall balcony jewel-mirror
    of Shahjehan the flowerhanded
        mad Hindoo-Arab smiler
Pursing flower in hand before his face the smile
    flitting on his princely lip —
Imprisoned bankrupt before he built
    his Black Taj across the river
connected with a Golden Bridge


— "Communist leader attacks China full faith in Nehru's
leadership
    Concern over slow economy progress Revenue board criti-
cized" — the Delhi Statesman scratching the human belly —
    My eyelids close on the book, the Morphine is late in the
night and the Ma announces echo call of nights before & Jai
Gagadam?! Jai
    Ganapatti to whom I prayed to remember & write his adven-
tures on his big rat on the planet
    before I wrote my name Ginsberg on my forhead in his Pro-
tective Bhang-day festival with postoffices closed & nothing
less than death or
    More than life possible in this here Coney Universe that re-
peats its possible Self over & over all the same boat and corpse
returning cow
    Shape Moo-Shabdh Hap of Locust Kalpas in their Shantih
roar
    comfortable money & behind untouched but only the thumb
on the pen burnt by cigarettes
    & index forefinger dream-stain of smoking hot tobacco exces-

185

sive & thin Bidi lung-cough — and
the fumes of the pipe spread in heard air — I shake my head
no & yes
Eyesed clothed speechless Guru thrilled ghat light — ah well.
* * *

*4 AM*
Rickshaw to Luxa, Gopinath Kovirag —
Three morns ago thru the barred window
his popeyed "no" sitting
as dozing I stared — disturbing his Prayer —
A moddle of Universes
floating upside down in
the vast in fact endless
Nothing
except this eyelip lowering
on spring-marble temple floors
Rickshaw to Lolark Kund asleep —
Asi Ghat closed shutters —
Namwar Singh alley
Colorless & no answer window
He just wanted to die.
He was thin & his skin
covered his bones like a
fat-ass glove —
with a rump burp —
Om Shanti
* * *
Explanation of Mysterious Words in *Aether*

ShàBà — Corpse (Bengali)
daha — burning (Sanscrit)
Sabadaha — Bengali pron. of Sanscrit
Shawadaha — burning of dead body — Sanskrit
abadie — locality, inhabitation
(Persian) place

— — —

Sabahadabadie — also in Hindi

186

                Saba — all, whole
                hadh — (Arabic) Limit
                badie — pharsi — badness
        Set a limit to all Evil
        _____|
                                                |       Poet
Aether — See Prajna-Upanishad                   |   Trilochan
                                                |   Shastri
                                                |       Explained
                                                |       this to me
*See AETHER poem lines 5 28 '60 "Old Hindu Sabahadabadie-*
*pluralic universes . . . moonlit towers . . ."*
                        * * *

"O go way man I can
    hypnotize dis nation
I can shake de earth's foundation
    with the maple leaf rag"
        — Maple Leaf Rag Song (1903)
                    * * *

*Fragment of long dream poem*
        Outmans paint the nabby wave
        in the stained blue canvas sheet

this the 4th stanza, mainly it was about
eternity etc. & in the dream writing rapidly
on a paper I remarked to myself that at last
I had found a simple foursquare verseform
that wasn't too demonstratively eccentric
& was able to be simple & write itself
easily & say anything — 4 line stanza

Wrenched myself out of sleep state to get
it written but lost a few words delayed
not realizing I wasn't still awake & not
opening my eyes.   Probably was writing
in the dream, thinking I was writing with
the scratchy pen & paper, only to find
I was *still* eyes closed adream

                    187

*March 8, 1963 —*

Walking long road at sunrise after sleep in room with (Delhi-Peking) Peace Marchers on blankets & rugs, vegetable stew supper & mosquito nets, everybody with notebooks scribbling diaries & letters. Arrive in Raja's palace & settle on another rug after tea, Peter humming some rock & roll patting on rug.

———  ———  ———  ———

*4 PM —*
Dust in the village clearing by the sport field leaves falling down yellow flies buzzing over the orange robes of the shining skull Japanese Buddhist sitting with his fan-drum "I salute the Buddha within each sentient . . ." and Shankar Rao Dev an old small man with snowy fur on skullcap & chin lifting his finger — microphone help held up below his chin from white seated sitter on ground — he in wool sweater & white pants pleading with villagers till he ends they applaud — Scott leaning in green chair on the canvas rug over the dust — I sitting high & depressed that they talk and who knows what to say — about China? about walking, falling leaves? The whistle of Microphone. Congress hats on head, fat local helpers from the Parties of Politics squat on thighs behind him. Several old spinners of wool with spindles and threads elongating in the air. The darker sky of late afternoon. An eyeglassed man in white clean creamy turban holds handkerchief to nose in audience — the thousand flies settle on white shirts — a few white caps splattered with early Holi holiday colored-dust waters — out thru the trees an earlier century gate & dome — Reading a paper question — "Will Mao help you to enter?" He raises his hands he don't know and answers from Gita. If God Wills. Around the ground seated a hundred or more, on the striped canvas covered with small yellow crisp leaves of early summer — a line of rows horseshoed around standing & listen, watching the Spiel.

Early this morn the American (Lazar) in Blue trembling explaining to the audience of school children. Someone stepped on my toe & broke an old scab open.

———  ———  ———

Trouble with Indian C.I.D. — Huxley warns against overpopulation — "Death control" —

*March 20, 1963*

Walking at night on asphalt campus
road by the German Instructor with Glasses
W.C. Williams is dead he said in accent
under the trees in Benares; I stopped and asked
Williams is Dead?    Enthusiastic and wide-eyed
under the Big Dipper.    Stood on the Porch
of the International House Annex bungalow
insects buzzing round the electric light
reading the Medical obituary in Time.
"out among the sparrows behind the shutters"
Williams is in the Big Dipper.    He isn't dead
as the many pages of words arranged thrill
with his intonations the mouths of meek kids
becoming subtle even in Bengal.    Thus
there's a life moving out of his pages; Blake
also "alive" thru his experienced machines.
Were his last words anything Black out there
in the carpeted bedroom of the gabled wood house
in Rutherford?    Wonder what he said,
or was there anything left in realms of speech
after the stroke & brain thrill-doom entered
his thoughts?    If I pray to his soul in Bardo Thodol
he may hear the unexpected vibration of foreign mercy.
Quietly unknown for three weeks; now I saw Passaic
and Ganges one, consenting his devotion,
because he walked on the steely bank & prayed
to a Goddess in the river, that he only invented,
another Ganga-Ma.    Riding on the old
rusty Holland submarine on the ground floor
Paterson Museum instead of a celestial crocodile.
Mourn O Ye Angels of the Left Wing! that the poet
of the streets is a skeleton under the pavement now

189

and there's no other old soul so kind and meek
and feminine jawed and him-eyed can see you
What you wanted to be among the bastards out there.
— — —
Make up your mind Mosquitoes buzzing
round my naked chest white sheet —
the brown hues of death's music vibration
Bam the mosquito suspended before my eye
and my tiny enemy dead on my palm
Several claps of memory jungle gyre back
to the Father's voice "You be a mosquito too"
"to be god" — alright, strike — merely my
awareness will keep them away — as he
buzzes circling in to my hair — as if
I were dead — and the rat cheeps in the wall —
Pinch in my neck, the nasty creatures minute
bloodsucking cannibal transparent vultures
circling over Peter's yellow mountainside of hair —
Williams can you hear me now?   Can you see
this blue page, the big dipper have you
a telescope.   I'll take Heisenberg for example.
The very act of writing creates emotion.
A locked door and the sound voices intoning
in the street by the Kali Mandir — Disturbs
the thought Process and so arrives at
its own abstract Nothing and Squiggle
of penmark symbols on Hieroglyph-paper
redbound book — A mirror for Auden
to see his long hand — Who praised Williams
on Ischia quoting Eliot, the late stroke poems
— which gossip I brought to that fringed couch
on the floor of the front windowed Room — Williams
pointing out the window "There's a lot of
bastards out there" — that's what he had to say;
and I said nothing, embarrassed and proud —
all poets drinking wine — "But what about
Angelhair?"   Gregory slunched in couch wide

staring eyebrows heavy with Vermouth — Jack said
gossiping in the kitchen 1920 Bavarian beergarden
love romance evening music under the linden trees
or some little haiku with lights and dancing
couples by the white fence and table.   I'm all off
— memories of Williams "I'll never see you again"
by his garden gate long long ago — The next time
"Lots of young poets interested in your asshole"
A poem he never wrote, Kavi Guru —
Master of the sweet Sadhana Ah! the rubber
Chand — The Mullah chanting on the Mosque
Tower — Ganja makes me write
tho the writing seems self important
disconnected and useless as per theory
Examination impedes function for a fraction
of a second, and the thoughts fly past
the selection a matter of memory as the
hand plies the pen to itself on the page
and makes a physical point  ⟶  •
that's a beginning.   What if my consciousness
were never to deviate from that first
succinct dot, telling the little there is to say,
I am here at the moment, smoking a cigarette.
Continuing out from there How are we going
to live in this Universe What is the question?
"Mind travels in space.   Bring it back to the center
of the lotus — itself Christ-Atman — from Siberia
or wherever you're thinking of," and bring
it back to this filling moving (when I
write it) page, following the words that
occur in the mind — excluding the
sounds that quote themselves interrupting
for some seconds to think their verbal
equivalent in picture — the Shady Street
at 5 AM the Milk Shop and Kali chapel
open and voices coming thru the shutter-doors
singing barking squealing and intoning humans

praying to God — That's a far cry! — the States on
the radio and a holy bell — singing the Ramayana
perhaps, I hear that voice warbling outside from below.
That mosquito again, buzzing round my pen clip
reflecting the ceiling bulb in polished yellow metal
penguin nose.    Penguin books is going to publish
this slush.    Why be self denying?    Say what you
Will.    Associate on the process of Association —
Have to look up to do that, like a sketcher staring
at the clothes hung over the chair at my desk
red robes and towel and blue shirt — Back not
to the lotus but the Bookpage now full —
Reader, please excite my attention and ask
the first question.    Who are you?    What
do you want.    What makes you think you're
going to get it this way.    What Good will it do?
I walked on the Delhi Peking Peace March
but have to advertise it myself this way —
my own private telegraph network — for power?
What would *I* do with the world?    What
suggestion can I make, calmly, to solve the
"World problem."    Join Communist?    Avenge
Lumumba, that's good.    That satisfied the F.B.I.
Join the F.B.I.?    Wouldn't be accepted.
So what good is the F.B.I. to me?    It's a
closed corporation, Government is big corporation,
I'm just poor poet me — I can say that without
much fear contradiction.    Arise ye prisoners
of Starvation!    How many of such Me or Me-ness
still exists?    In every clime from Pole to China —
So therefore there must be a big conspiracy
to close off this Me and put Them
up in power or if I was them in Power
I would also be closed in by certain
necessities of Power?    No I would take
off my close & go naked on Television
with Kruschev — have to set up a

mutual Government before that, so nobody
watching would seize power — on Mescaline —
Everybody could see in their homes National Holiday
or rule that everybody had to appear on television,
if at all, Naked.   But the great Hunger of the
Undeveloped Nations.   Give China your Wheat and
Machines, America.   But how ever recreate India?
Bang Bang Bang continues the bronze gong of Kali
downstairs.   Well its flowing fast enough &
oddly conditioned but my eyelids are heavy
from 4 AM Ganja and I need an excuse to sleep.

*Sun 10 AM Mar 24, 1963 —*

Wrote Bill long letter & all night up at Ghats, a black skull
hanging down the end of the wood bed — Peter asleep on Ghat
Curled up in wooden perch on stone platform — back here
turned on & wrote till morning — lay down to read it afterward
& on first page closed my eyes "I'm with you at your side" — "I
was with you at your side" — "I was at your side all the time"
Bill's voice at the typewriter.
* * *

> Illustrious object balloon igloo
>> Select Toulouse Lautrec
> Connection with ding a ling and
>> echo of hundredcaved
> hungry mourners on the ghat,
>> sleeping in heat night
> on the nod my face
>> wakes with a smile
> voices chirping and shouting &
>> remembering mosquito to Sarod
> Sparrows in the eaves I think
>> I dropped my split pea
>> Borsht Soup — the
>>> tin
>>> Emperor's Halls
* * *

193

Went to Khajuraho — nice trees and temples & crickets on
ganja — disaffected and Peter brusque all week — woke this
morning thinking of God & having read Bankey Behari's Sufi
Poets last nite the whiff of Springtime tho its beginning summer
in Benares the instant I woke on the floor with Market voices &
children exclaiming all around a lotus of sound — My cigarette
cough & the body decay lungs taste bad — Where am I in wil-
derness? Now at present the peculiar summery Nostalgia —
Childhood feel — Empty lots & Diner backyards in Paterson
      Wandering lonesome by hedges —
      Burroughs' Music down windy
      street — Mouth tastes bad, smoke —
      Committing lung suicide with cigarettes
      Some morning I'll wake up like this
      & be doomed realizing cancer chest —
                    * * *
The Sun is
on the horizon
burning Arab Circle
         bearded with white clouds
Zigzag few cracks of lightning
         from the bright pupil

      — daydream picture in minds eye on morphine.
                    * * *

194

Should they ask him back, where could he come
The newspapers would scream attack again
Poor once child Charlie with white white hair
roaming alone on Hollywood's crummy streets
Norma Talmage dead, all his old enemies dead,
Hearst's wrinkles turned to dust & Louella & Hedy
Senile cardplayers in Texicon swimmingpools
Underwater trading ghosted autobiographies
Nothing but thin film of acrid smog level
of the roofs, cars swifting by & bus snorts
and strangers on the pave in checked suits
selling universe insurance — even if he walked Mustached
and baggy pantsd nobody'd notice, nobody'd
give him a dime & the police wouldn't agree —
Hollywood is changed & dry & Chaplin's old wet nose
smells Switzerland at the end of the collossal
Sweet dream all alone, the big city's vanished
and radar makes the traffic lites blink green & red.
All the old Directors houses with tennis trees
and swimming pools lined with butlers &
Mahogany huge rooms sit in Space, dusty
and poor Charlot w/a million dollars in
his baggy trousercuffs wanders aimlessly
down Vine looking for his ancient Studio roofs
and his dead Jewish Cameraman Stravinsky
Sits around retired smoking cigars by his grandchild's
girlish coffin & the world is finished with Me.
1920's America vanished into crackly rolls
of celluloid, the big green hugewheeled car
with neat black canvas roof — Even Buster Keaton
got rheumatism and can't fall down off ladders
into the grave without staying there forever anymore —
Beatnicks & Electronic workers collect paychecks
in Straub's Drug store and what plump breasted
little girl wants to sleep with a part in the pix
because the television hustlers in sharkskin hips
with unwrinkled laps full of Zippers are too flip

to fuck for romantic fun in front of the late late show.
Charlie'd be Charlie lonely at last
and realize even his mustached genius film
forgotten & the depression talkies buzzing & zapping
in flashes of blue light under the pavements radiostore.

\* \* \*

*Dream* —
We are on Small town radio — FM in Hotel & interviewed by
fat man — Peter in course of conversation says "Well, there's
injustice... didn't Churchill Winston Churchill murder people"
— Everybody gasps "& he probably did I dunno —" — The fat
announcer says, "Well that is your opinion" — I let it ride, it's
the second time Peter's insulted Churchill — Everybody in the
small upstairs studio is jittery — the walrus mustached announcer says we "ought to leave in case *they* come" — I start to
leave but then feel that's cowardly we ought to straighten this
out in advance but I don't want to intrude on Peter & same time
afraid we'll be arrested for slander. We leave — guiltily — down
the stairs, I expect the worst.

\* \* \*

*Dream* —
In Supermarket a big green blue moon in the sky descending
larger & larger, with colored rings, it must be Saturn — it's an
object like a flying Saucer? — No it's bigger maybe whole of
Saturn coming close —
I'm watching with a girl — it's descending over the roofs,
down the long avenue behind the parking lot of the Supermarket
— bigger & bigger till it's big as a bus it finally
Settles down outside the window right near where I'm watching, a sort of flashbulb light brightness against it & it's revealed
in the lightningstroke instant — a big busfull of Tibetan Monks
just floated down from the sky on a parachute — What an
amazing Holiday Surprise they pulled on everybody — I wonder who saw & what they intended to mean — I rush out to the
curb — the bus immediately starting up begins to pull away,
they're not going to wait an instant but speed back to Head-
quarters, it's all organized on the splitsecond — They in their

196

bus vanishing down the block — I rush out & seeing that they're Tibetan monks, am delighted, & thinking nobody understood their special gesture but me, I bow Chinese style to them, I bow and bow — they all rise up instantly at once, within the bus, and bow back to me as the bus speeds off down the Long Island highway — 6 lanes in front of Eugene's Hicksville supermarket at night — They all speed off bowing with Mongol-Tibetan cheeks gleaming in the yellow light — I bow again happily, they bow, I got their message, what a wierd idea to float down in a baloon-bus & speed away not waiting for explanations just to show that you are the Saturnal Forces already here on Earth.

*April 7, '63 —*

Waking mid afternoon, day wasted idly — weeks passing idly —

The man dying covered with sweat his thin stick arms & legs corpse stretched out on the Ghat under the Tree — Prasad's Kankal — I gave him 2 1/2 cents — all week watching him waste away & bleed from bony hips —

The two American boys who slept on floor, their Billy Bud twin innocence, search outside of America to see the life of people.

\* \* \*

The beggar all week under the green giant tree
in the iron fenced beggar-Sadhu-sleepers
half naked-leper Park Deshbandu's statue
at the end of the green triangle — the beggar
made of bones with brown skin stretched
and white-sored buzzing with flys near
the prune asshole in the valleys of meatless
pelvis bonecap, his sharp shoulders and
naked horny hip bleeding red drops, lying
in the white sun face covered with sweat
teeth poked familiar thru — long cheeks &
black eyes dimned two days with sick
grey rheum and backbone sharp as a big

197

fish spine grinding against the dry asphalt
near the wall concrete urinal by the ally
corner where dusty garbage barrows, steel
lip to the ground empty or filled with black
dirt & dead vegetable dogs, rest the night —

The beggar — the Kankal man — skeleton
perched squatting tall on his wasted skinny legs
and big feet, his brown lingam hung to earth still
fat huge worm — drinking red claycup of Milk
with hard bread — hip sores a feast for black
buzzing circle of eaters flies, he droop lidded
indifferent squinting black cheeked, he breathing stretched out
head in the gutter long arms and legs brown tendons
stretched skin — Buttocks no hollows in the place where
he sits on his spine and thin stick thighs — or legs
drawn to chest balanced on long feet, lifted into crossleg
for support lying down at ease unconscious or asleep —
after Milk, he asked for bread — Dipped the sweet
crust in the hot milk — that Shit all over two puddles
nearby and a splat of smelly brown mud on
the burlap pillow of the ashy longhaired Sadhu grey-man
floating on spread rags near — his neighbor's lost body
— and the dwarf-legged splay-hoofed fourfoot
cripple grey dung-plastered cow his acquaintance
companying him — One afternoon slept head on
the cowside resting — several days his guardian
over dogs — And the naked leperlady like a
romantic dry brown plum nearby quavering
helplessly, clean thumbless palms and grey
fingerstumps — that all nite tonite I heard
whooping a dwoodling yoop in the soprano
throat-back I thought cancer madness choir call —
not yet dead, recovering balancing day by day,
not speaking.
　　　　　　　He after predawn milk
spilled by a puppy sniffing eager his rag knee
— asked for cloth for his legs and belly hollow

writing "pyjamas" in the dust in Hindi letters,
could not speak — yet last night heard
his squeals of love height — I thought
death pains but as I came to his skeleton
flat on back with open eyeballs white, heeled
his voice to impersonal wail-whoop and nodded
as I said *Namaste* with adoring palms
joined at my chest.

*Bodh Gaya April 14? ('63) —*

Death is not a single thing.

— — —

    Morning — woke in Mahabodi Society Bldg — fan turning
high ceilings — a cough — mosquitoes rare last nite — itch,
Scabies returned — a cold, in lungs phlegm — my toe sore,
second toe nicked constantly — slight sore throat — eyes
blurred & smarting from acromyacin from conjunctivitis —
smoking cough & lungs retched — hack — agh —
    Dream — a tall man in the dream skating to Australia or
chasing around on Dodgems from Cony Island playland —
eitherway, a mirrorlike surface for the ground, sea or tin —
something happened I don't remember — a tall figure in a suit
like at Rockerfeller Center the Radioannouncer — Nowhere.
    Worrying about drugs, lsd. Should I take or not.

— — — — — — —

    Last nite under the Bo tree, Stars, the square pointy temple.

\* \* \*

*Rajgir: Dream —*
Taxicab with Peter going up modern street as in a previous
dream existence — the place is a big park on the left trees and
grass for blocks on the right a band of greenery & fields leading
to the river, as perhaps Chicago —
    In the taxi — we have just eaten in the Ordona restaurant or
the Miro Cardona restaurant — or we have an old apartment in
the Miro Cardona Apts or we live on Ordona Circus — We are
in a taxi speeding up Broadway to the hotel — It's just an acci-

dent we're living there, I think to myself — only I wish Leroi
Jones didn't know about that in the dream — I'm not sure what
my sin is — but it's numbered by Ordona —

Now that we're in familiar territory up on Broadway it seems,
I want to stop the cab & get a maybe trolley or subway — we're
just coming home from a ship or airplane — but Peter, with
whom I am not talking that afternoon, says "Ordona" to the
Taximan so that we speed all the way uptown into the Two
Dollar taxi-meter zone — But time is money, so we'll get home
faster — he has work to do, several letters to send off immediately, that has to be taken care of, I envisage his four air letters
all prepared to be signed —

The new apartment we live in is very polished & modern and
suave — mahogany sideboards and window frames & a folding
bed that comes down from the wall. We're home & we're in bed
together — tho it is not Peter any more, but a slightly younger
tougher young kid — some grocer's delivery boy Indian —
rather like Gopal the orphan saint of Deshbandu Leper's Park
in Benares —

He has just finished some sort of puja, worship & prayers
ceremony with others in the room who have left and we are together alone for the first time in bed. We're discussing "Wung"
initiation Diksha and he's been initiated —

"Well I've not been initiated" I say.

"That's alright" he says reaching for some dirt from a flower-
pot, & he puts a tilak 3rd eye on my forehead with his thumb.

"But can you give that initiation too?" I say submitting
myself to his hands

"Well I have given this mark to you & I've given it to others
too and I have the power to do that, tho I'm not certain you'd be
satisfied it's a formal initiation. Still I've been initiated and
that's good enough. Just accept whatever comes your way"

We're in bed and he's hovering over me, I have my head
between his knees, lying there — My leg or my cheek on his
thighs — I close my eyes and begin to feel a wavy soft friendli-
ness from him — my own sensuality of wet dreams coming in
my legs & breast — "Is *this* the excitement of initiation?"

200

"Well if that's what you're feeling that's your own so why not accept it?"

I think, well this is fine, but I am a little scared of spoiling the circumstance by making erotic scenes with him, reaching up & kissing his cheek & touching his thighs — I'm getting old — still he's here in bed — Who is he? —

"But am I supposed to act this out & feel this way"

"Why not? Do you see anything wrong?"

I have feeling I'm being trapped, meanwhile the blind wave of love is growing stronger & I don't want to resist —

"Well Teacher I'd be happy if this were the teaching, It's my old habit anyway — but I feel this may be a distracting test, & not the right manner of teaching?"

"Whatever you feel, as your heart tells you"

"But my heart tells me twice differently — on one hand the old lovely sensual temptation of Ordona Apartments — But flesh is crawling & unpermanent you know it says here" —

"Yes that's true too" —

"So that while pleasurable it may be a little childish"

And as I say that line & realised it seems it is childish to make this initiation a love scene —

I wake up. Not sure, but the love softness persists after the dream.

*Vulture Peak — Rajgir April 18, 1963 —*

## GRIDHAKUTA HILL

I've got to get out of the sun
mouth dry and red towel wrapped
      round my head
walking up crying singing *ah sunflower*
*Where the traveller's journey*
closed my eyes *is done* in the
      black hole there
      sweet rest far far away
up the stone climb past where
Bimbisara left his armies
got down off his elephant
and walked up to meet
Napoleon Buddha pacing
      back and forth on the platform
      of red brick on the jut rock crag
Staring out Lidded-eyed beneath
the burning white sunlight
down on Rajgir kingdom below
    ants wheels within wheels of empire
    houses carts streets messengers
      wells and water flowing
      into past and future simultaneous
      kingdoms here and gone on Jupiter
distant X-ray twinkle of the eye
myriad brick cities on earth and under
New York Chicago Palenque Jerusalem
      Delphos Macchu Picchu Acco
        Herculaneum Rajagriha
here below all windy with the tweetle
    of birds and the blue rocks
      leaning into the blue sky —
Vulture Peak desolate bricks

flies on the knee hot shadows
    raven-screetch and wind blast
      over the hills from desert plains
        south toward Bodh Gaya —
All the noise I made with my mouth
singing on the path up, Gary
Thinking all the *pale youths*
and *virgins shrouded with snow*
chanting Om Shantih all over the world
    and who but *Peter du Peru*
walking the streets of San Francisco
    arrived in my mind on Vulture Peak
Then turned round and around on my heels
singing and plucking out my eyes
ears tongue nose and balls as I whirled
longer and longer the mountains stretched
    swiftly flying in circles
the hills undulating and roads speeding
    around me in the valley
    Till when I stopped the earth
      moved in my eyeballs
    green bulges slowly
        and stopped . . .
My thirst in my cheeks and tongue
    back throat drives me home.
        \* \* \*

*April?* —
*Nalanda* — Dream — Flying round the world I reach Paris or
New York, Bill is in room with clippings of Time Magazine &
Gysin — he has new method which infuriated the Critics or
Bourgeois or someone or me or the *Artistes* are angry again &
he's sitting there happily snarling sneers of glee in his suite in
mid room — I don't understand it all no more & feel left out &
I go to Austria feeling depressed.

    Bill reading a clipping of opposition, in grey suit — it's a
European City — perhaps a cut-up of the Dharma — a cut-up
of the 4 Noble Truths in fact? — or else a cut-up of Einstein —

It's irritated some sector of the community like the American Scientists Right Wing & they're protesting.

*Dream 23 April 1963 —*

News story with banner-long headline on inner front page of Telegram: "Author Sells to Make Tax Gain Compensation" or something technical to do with taxes — Regarding Burroughs — the story goes on to quote "So it's the niggers & reds & pinks & Chinks gonna be our friend in the end against the Jupiter Cancer Virus Armies we better get on kissen Cousin terms with Mao-Ma. . . The army needs Fairies & The Navy needs Lesbians in this Emergency Stopgap" etc — long outrageous statements which make sense: it seems he made the papers by selling some verb invention like the cut ups.

I'm looking at it with my father, & show him & say "You see Burroughs will now is now having a liberalizing influence on the fucking country" — and Louis rather passively nods "yes" — I go away realizing what a good job Bill has done — tho I'm troubled by having said fucking country that is a little odd — In the paper the small photo with eyes 👀 looking up, right rather funny a *Lee* look, neat with executive bow-tie.

\* \* \*

*Patna* — The Prakritic echo of Golghar\*
          circling round the concrete dome
          as I recited the sun flower
          hearing my own voice sadly
          echo, tired thousand miles.

\* \* \*

*Patna-Benares Express 4/63*

Whatever it may be whoever it may be
The bloody man all singing all just
However he die
He rode on railroad cars

---

\* A stone dome for grain storage, 19th century British construction.

He woke at dawn, in the white light of a new universe
He couldn't do any different
He the skeleton with eyes
raised himself from a wooden bench
felt different looking at the fields and palm trees
Empty hearted with no love child in his future
no money in the bank of dust
no nation but the inexpressible grey clouds before sunrise
lost his identity cards in his wallet
in the bald rickshaw by the Maidan in dry Patna
Stared hopeless waking from drunken sleep
dry mouthed in the RR Station
among the sleeping shoeshine men in loincloth on the dirty
    concrete
Too many bodies thronging these cities now

—— —— ——

Realize either way with friends
listening to his last whispers
by the covers in the bedroom
or alone staring at a strange
        Streetcorner hospital
            wall,
The same nowhere to go.

                * * *

"Without regard to the fruits of action"
"In this universe pervaded by Speech & Mind ... The Lord
    Ganesha is above Speech & Mind."

*Dream May 1, 1963 —*

Kajuraho style, I'm holding a baby boy in my arms and he's
seated on my biceps — I'm blowing him, his Cock in my mouth,
adoration in the dream — Peter nearby standing.

*Morning Dream — May 3, 1963*

Little Vijyashankar the Brahmin landlord's boy who comes &
sits on our bed came & woke me. I went back to sleep — in dream

he climbed over my body, and finally settled along the front of my bulk, nestling near my loins.

"Guru Guru Guru Guru Guru Guru Guru" as per Citaram Onkar Das Thakur (Mantra for finding Guru, 2 weeks continuous repetition no sex meat onions smoke.)

*May 13, 1963 — 6 AM — Part of a Dream —*

I go out and walk on the main crowd-thronged boardwalk — as in India in Allahabad at Magh Mela, mopy grey robed holymen & asses & mules and cows and barbers squatting on the roadway & ring of rickshaw bells.

Passing a garbage disposal mound on streetcorner I see a horse leaned over forward about to collapse, with its left hind leg all bone & pink under tissue rotten, eaten away, stretched back just about on last legs for balancing, but the head stretched forward into the garbage moving jaws slowly feebly eating — as I walk ahead and look back the horse looks almost normal except for that rotten back leg. I'd seen him in dream before too.

*May 13 —*

6 AM the yellow sun outside balcony thru the trees Dasaswamedh ghat waking up with Rickshaw bells — I been in bed several days with kidney troubles — Hay Ram Ram Hay — sings the Motley-clad-in-yellow-and-orange Medieval Clown-looking Bhakta who every day passes clanging his little cymbals to his ears, his head turned aside to listen to the Sound — singing in melancholy continuous rhythm Hey Ram Ram Hey with a falling tone of voice ending each announcement, as he walks in circles or stops to listen to himself sing in the street approaching the steps down to the river — That I've seen him often each day for months — once offered him some change, thinking him a beggar, which he refused.

*May 14 —*

Peter packing up to move to another room in Bengali Tola.

*May 19, 1963 —*

Now alone in the bare whitewashed black floored room in
Benares with the surf noise of cows drums and bycicles mur-
mering on the street — this room a quiet one-night cave emptied
of the furniture — a few unwanted relics left behind the Ganesh-
red painted marriage pot for water cooling beneath the table a
few bricks and bottles of red medicine half empty — Peter gone
to sleep the night in his new room in an alley a mile away down
Bengali Tola, we held hands a moment I said goonight honey
after several weeks strained halting conversation — I about to
leave for Japan — America, Peter wearing a pink lungi rayon
skirt, bare chested with his carryall cotton bag hung on his
shoulder and close cropped hair walking barefoot past the Kali
display booth temple & the cigarette stall around the corner into
the alley on his way home to sleep in solitude, and I to the river
to wash my hands & pour water on head & glance at the fires of
Manikarnika Ghat faraway an instant before coming upstairs
to face the — to stand in the bare room my last night here —
putting out white & brown dysentery pills and laying at my
bedside a copy of Blake & notebook & handkerchief & cigarettes
and Newsweek & Times of India & ashtray and rubber sandals
— My bed reduced to a blanket on warm black stone floor and
a sheet & airmattress pillow to recline on — Peter's excellent
red clay ganesh with bellybuttons & finely painted white elephant head sitting guard over the french door in an alcove —
a Hindi alphabet sheet I never learned from much, hung on the
wall by what was the kitchen table crowded with baskets of
fruit cucumbers oranges lemons bananas and potatoes we cooked
on small tin kerosine stove now removed & floor swept — Peter
forgot the mirror — he'll come in the morn to take — I'll wake
at dawn take bath downstairs on river steps — Now what to do
with this familiar melancholy but salute the burning ghats? —
   Remembering many scenes I never wrote of — The fate of the
Kankal Skeleton we fed & washed under the pepal tree by the
green ganja sadhu leper's park by the market downstairs — His

207

brother came from Delhi with 20 yr old pants & mustache & I saw him off on the train yesterday —

The odd Jester of the streets who passed under balcony daily — I could hear his characteristic rapid clang clang of finger cymbals as he walked quick stepped, sometimes turning around on his heels to all directions, his head cocked aside eyes distracted quietly as he listened to his own cling cling near his ear & sang repeatedly continuously day after day month by month Ram Nam Hey! Hey Ram Nam! Ram Nam Hey! — with white leggings & chain of bells around his front and striped apron & yellow shirt & orange towel, his thin face topknotted with black Sikh hair & black beard raised to one side his head tilted listening to his cymbals & whirling every so often around to the sky & balconies saying  Ram's Nam Hey! —

Another more stout Harlequin Sadhu — with bells on ankles & around belly & many orange robes & cloths & turbans & small rag bag over shoulder who I often saw walking shuffling actually very regularly like an express train so his bells all over rang repeatedly regularly rhythm of his up-street shuffle — with a grey woman Schoolteacherish face & very kindly — he'd march clinging-chimingly up past the Ghandi-ashram Kali shop stoop & stop at a child with his sadhu arm up holding a bowl of 3rd eye forehead powder, anoint the child & smile & move on in his ragged dignified perpetual motley bellsound shuffle.

The sentinal sadhu at the corner of the park always there with kindly eye begging & his singsong Jai Raaam extended his hands clasped bowing at me as I passed echoing his Jai Ram —

All month since I came back from Bodh Gaya Peter unwelcoming & silent & determined on his separate music & untouchable energies — slow drift to we silent & curt answers, neither raising voice in my sadness or he in his irritation and no long talk except one night on Morphine he telling me I'm washed up & sold out to go teach in Vancouver broken poetry vow he judged — I had nothing to say, being washed up desolate on the Ganges bank, vegetarian & silent hardly writing & smoking no pot except many leters & kidney attacks don't care. Still this melancholy aloness is like returning home.

Anyway the silent time in this room reaching back to 1943, saying farewell to the hallway of Divinity Dormitory in N. York where I first saw L . . . . . & Jack.

Now all personal relations cold exhausted.

I'll be on impersonal curiosity hence flying round the world hoping for not.

Street noises & snorting of bulls rising to climax & sticks whacked on the road below the open window thru the branches of the tree I see the night street crowded with dog barks — some bulls are hitting each other with their heads & pushing & snorting.

The other night chorus of twenty lame dog barks rising & making symphony together angry at perhaps a cow. One night they all yowled together melancholy music different dog wail notes climaxing under the full moon — last week.

*May 22, 1963 Last Night in Calcutta —*

Still night.   The old Clock ticks,
half past two.   A ringing of crickets
awake in the ceiling.   The gate is locked
on the street outside — sleepers, mustaches,
nakedness, but no desire.   A few mosquitoes
waken the itch, the fan turns slowly —
a car thunders along the black asphalt,
a bull snorts, something is expected —
Time sits solid in the four yellow walls.
Train whistles call answer to the horned
beast.   No one is here, emptiness filled
with dog barks, answered a block away.
Pushkin sits in the bookshelf, Shakespere's
complete works as well as Blake's unread —
O Spirit of Poetry, no use calling on you
babbling in this emptiness furnished with beds
under the bright oval mirror — perfect
night for sleepers to dissolve in tranquil
blackness, and rest these eight hours

— Waking to stained fingers, bitter mouth
and lung gripped by cigarette hunger,
what to do with this big toe, this arm,
this eye in the starving skeleton filled
sore-horse tramcar heated Calcutta in
Eternity — sweating and teeth rotted away —
Rilke at least could dream about 'Lovers'
the old breast excitement and trembling belly,
is that it?   And there's the vast space & stars —
If the brain changes matter breathes
fearfully back on man — But now
the great crash of building and planets
breaks thru the walls of language and drowns
me under its Ganges heaviness forever.
No escape but thru Bankok & New York to Death.
But that would only close the dream
in the old know box.   Light multiplies
light to the fast bong of father clocks.
Skin is sufficient to be skin, that's all
it ever could be, tho screams of pain in the kidney
make it sick of itself, a hollow dream
dying to finish its all too famous misery
— leave immortality for another to suffer like a fool,
not get stuck in a corner of the Universe
sticking morphine in the arm and eating meat.

*Bankok — May 28, '63*

Chinese meats hanging in shops — . . .

* * *